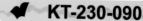
Name:	Anisha Mistry (I do have a middle name but it's too embarrassing so am **NOT** writing it here)
Age:	10 years, 3 months and 10 days (at time of writing this)
Lives with:	Mum, Dad, and my mischievous Granny Jas
School:	Birmingham South-West Aspire Junior Middle High Academy School (longest school name ever!)
Favourite Subject:	Science
Best friend:	Milo Moon
Ambitions:	To meet a real life astronaut
	To invent a cure for meanness
	To be the first kid in space

For Deepak who believed I could.
SERENA

For the sisters of The South Room for their wise counsel, cat photos, nephew videos, and excellent giffage. You keep me sane.
EMMA

First published in the UK in 2021 by Usborne Publishing Ltd., Usborne House, 83-85 Saffron Hill, London EC1N 8RT, England, usborne.com

Usborne Verlag, Usborne Publishing Ltd., Prüfeninger Str. 20, 93049 Regensburg, Deutschland VK Nr. 17560

Text copyright © Serena Patel, 2021

Illustrations copyright © Usborne Publishing Ltd., 2021

Illustrations by Emma McCann.

The name Usborne and the Balloon logo are Trade Marks of Usborne Publishing Ltd.

A CIP catalogue record for this book is available from the British Library.

JFMAM JASOND/22 ISBN 9781474959544 8794/1

Printed in India

ANISHA

ACCIDENTAL DETECTIVE

GRANNY
TROUBLE

SERENA PATEL

Illustrated by Emma McCann

USBORNE

CHAPTER ONE

ROAD TRIP!

"**ANISHA!** It's time to go! Come on, Dad's outside with the minibus!" Mum shouts from downstairs.

I close my eyes and take a deep breath. Okay, it won't be **that** bad. Will it? It's just me and my **entire** family, travelling to Leicester in a minibus and spending three days there. **Together.**

I check my bag one last time: notebook, pen, book on the history of space exploration. One more thing to add. I sit on the bed and pull open the drawer of my bedside table. There it is – my silver autograph book. It's one of the most special things I own. I flick through the pages. I've got autographs

and replies to my letters from the people I most
admire in here. Tim Berners-Lee – he invented the
internet. Brian Cox, the brilliant physicist, Tim
Peake, the astronaut, and Professor Dame Jocelyn
Bell Burnell – did you know she discovered radio
pulsars*?

* Pulsars are the remains of stars that have gone supernova
– which means they have exploded! You can sometimes see
them blinking in the sky from earth - so cool!

And this weekend I'm going to add Sangeeta Sanśōdhaka. She is a **famous** Indian space engineer. When I first read about her, I was so excited to see someone who looked like **me** doing my dream job. Then just last month, Milo and I **WON** the **National Schools Science Fair**. The prize is a trip to the National Space Centre in Leicester. We'll get to see actual rockets and space rovers, and by coincidence Sangeeta is going to be there too. She's in England for a conference and is doing some work with the Space Centre, so Milo and I will get to meet her in person! It's the most exciting thing ever to happen to me and I can't wait.

Mum and Dad and the rest of my family decided that, as we haven't been to Leicester for a long time and it's half-term, we should all go. The **ShabdKosh** festival happens in Leicester every year and it's taking place this weekend. **ShabdKosh** means "everything" and the festival literally contains **ALL** the things you could think of to do with

Indian culture and food. Granny has always wanted to go, but usually Dad's working or there's other stuff happening. This year, because of our prize, Dad took the time off so we can all go and make a little holiday of it. He's already calling it the **Mistrys' Road Trip Extravaganza**. I don't know why – Leicester's not *that* far away.

Anyway, the festival sounds kind of interesting, I guess. They're having a **Wonders of the World** theme this year and there are going to be some cool displays. Hopefully my family won't do what they usually do whenever we go anywhere and cause mayhem...

We're going to explore the festival for our first two days in Leicester, before I finally get to go to the Space Centre on Monday. It'll be fine, I tell myself. It's only nine of us staying in a little bed and breakfast, sharing rooms and being together every moment of **EVERY DAY**!

ME
+
MY FAMILY
x
3 DAYS
=
RECIPE FOR DISASTER!

"Anisha, how long does it take to get your things together? Come on now, beta, everyone is waiting!" Granny yells up the stairs.

I grab my bag and run down, only to find everyone **NOT** waiting, but still trying to get about a **hundred bags** in the big black minibus parked outside our house. Uncle Tony's limousine has pulled up behind it, its boot full of pink luggage that is being transferred into the minibus's large luggage compartment. It's already quite full, but Mum is desperately trying to fit another bag in by pushing it with her bum.

"You do know we're only going for a few days, right?" I say to her.

"They're not mine!" Mum huffs, out of breath. "It's all Bindi's. She must think we're **moving** to Leicester."

"I heard that!" protests Bindi from somewhere behind another pile of luggage on the pavement.

Just then Uncle Tony, who was leaning over into the back seat of the limo, stands up. He groans under the weight of the biggest make-up case I've ever seen.

"Sweetums, are you sure you need all this, my love?" he wheezes.

"Oh yes, honeykins, I only packed the bare minimum," Bindi squeals, taking the make-up case from him with no trouble at all.

"There had better be space for my tubs!" Granny pushes past both of them, carrying a **tower** of Tupperware.

"What on earth is all that for?" Mum asks.

"Well, I want to get some of that lovely Leicester food while we're there so I can freeze it when we get back. Plus, they've opened a new **Spice Bazaar** and Mrs Kumar from number 23 went last month and she came back with all sorts of delicious things. I can do my chopping and sorting in Leicester and have everything all neatly packed in my tubs for the journey home," Granny tells her happily.

Mum opens her mouth to say something but then seems to decide against it. When Granny Jas wants to do something, eventually we end up doing it, so the tubs get loaded on too.

My cousins Mindy and Manny are already in the minibus and wave at me through the window. I wave back. It's so nice now we're all **friends**. It hasn't always been that way, but I'm actually looking forward to spending some time with them this week.

"Hey, Neesh!" Milo makes me jump as he runs up behind me cheerfully. "I was worried you guys would go without me. I can't believe we're leaving so early. I'm usually still asleep at 7 a.m. on a Saturday."

"No chance of leaving you behind or leaving on time. We're still loading up," I say, nodding at the pile of bags that Uncle Tony, his chauffeur Mustaf, my mum and now Dad are trying to **squeeze** into the already full luggage compartment.

"This minibus is **sick**," Milo says, impressed.

"I've never been in one this **posh.**"

"Dad borrowed it from his friend who runs a coach company," I say. "It's really **swish** inside. I had a look last night when Dad brought it home."

"It's got a state-of-the-art **satnav**!" Dad grins as he passes us with another pink bag.

"Another bag?" huffs Tony. "You know, sweetums, we'll have no space for the clothes you want to buy in Leicester," he says to Aunty Bindi.

Aunty Bindi's head pops out from behind the minibus. "What!?" she exclaims in a high-pitched voice. "No, no, we must have space. I've got my eye on at least ten outfits from the new collections in my magazines." She points

glumly to the smallest case on the pile. "I mean, I suppose we can leave this behind."

Mustaf steps forward. "May I offer my **services**, madam? I could follow in the car with the remaining bags."

Aunty Bindi looks hopefully at Uncle Tony, but he shakes his head. "No, Mustaf. Thank you for offering but it's your week off and your family are expecting to see you. But you can help me in another way. Do you remember when I took the twins camping that one year?"

Mustaf smiles ever so slightly and nods.

"Didn't I buy a **ridiculously** big roof rack for that trip? I'm sure I still have it in the garage. Would you be able to drive round to the house quickly and bring it?" asks Uncle Tony.

"Of course!" Mustaf moves swiftly towards the limo, hops in and speeds off.

Aunty Bindi runs over to Uncle Tony and flings her arms around him. "Thank you, sweetums, I know

I'm a pain needing all my things with me," she says, smiling.

"Never a pain, my love." Uncle Tony smiles back at her, gooey-eyed. I have to look away before they start smooching. Grown-ups are so **yucky** sometimes.

Milo blushes, embarrassed by all the lovey-dovey stuff like me. **"ANYWAY!"** he practically shouts. "Neesh, I read up on the **Shabdkosh** festival your granny told us about. We are still going, aren't we? I can't wait, I've never been to a festival before! I've got my action-cam hat that Nan bought me for my birthday and I can record

EVERYTHING we see and do," he says, tapping the little square lens perched on top of his baseball cap.

"I'm not deaf, Milo, you don't need to **yell**. And to answer your question, yes, we are still **going** to the festival. If we ever get out of here, that is."

Mindy sticks her head out of the minibus window. "You know, Milo, they have a very famous **jewel** on display at the festival," she says, raising her eyebrows at us.

"Ooh, like **how** famous? Is it more famous than **David Attenborough**? Or more famous than the **dinosaurs**?" Milo asks.

"Technically, I don't know if you'd call dinosaurs famous, Milo," I say. "But I will tell you an interesting jewel fact. Diamonds are the only gem made up of a single chemical element. Isn't **THAT** more interesting than how famous something is?"

Milo looks at me for a moment, thinking. Then he turns back to Mindy and asks, "Mindy, is it more **famous** than Steve Backshall – you know, that animal guy off the telly? He swam with sharks!

Wait, I'm coming up, save me a seat by you so we can talk about it on the way!"

I smile, shaking my head.

Mum passes me with her long list. "Isn't it **exciting**, Anni? Lots of lovely quality **family time**. You can help me find all these special scented candles and incense sticks while we're there, if you like. There's a shop with all the best spiritual supplies. It'll be fun."

Just then Granny sneaks up on me – **she always does that**! She's wearing her favourite **salwar kameez** – the cream one with the green-and-pink patterned chunni*. She never wears a sari when we travel, as she says it's too difficult to use the toilet. I don't know what the difference is between using our toilet and one somewhere else, but that's **Granny logic** for you. "Are you getting on the bus or not, **beta**? Mustaf will be back any second and as

* A chunni is a headscarf, usually worn with a salwar kameez, which is a long tunic top and trousers. Granny says they're really comfortable. Whenever I've worn one, I usually end up losing my chunni or leaving it somewhere.

soon as that roof rack is loaded, we need to get moving."

I look at Granny grinning her gummy grin at me. "Granny, did you pack your **teeth**?"

"Oh, yes. I just don't like to wear them on long journeys. They rattle in my mouth when the road is bumpy," she replies.

"Oh, I see," I say, **wincing** at the thought. "Anyway, shall I check if Dad can fit your bag in the luggage compartment, Granny? I'm not sure there's enough space though. What on earth have you got in there?"

"I never go anywhere without my tongue scraper, my nail cutters and my calendar."

I smile, shaking my head. Granny is so strange sometimes. She puts her bag with the others and says, "Come on, **beta**, let's get on the minibus. I see Mustaf coming down the road."

I follow Granny onto the bus. There are five rows of seats – four to each row with an aisle down the middle. Dad is sitting in the driver's seat with Mum behind him. Manny's **proudly** sitting in the front passenger seat. He recently had a growth spurt so now he's allowed to sit in the front. Mindy wasn't happy at all because now Manny is taller than her! She said it was rude of Manny not to wait for her to grow too. They are twins after all! Milo and Mindy are sitting halfway back on the minibus.

I sit on the same row as them but on the other side of the aisle. I don't mind sitting by myself – it's nice to have some space for once. Granny sits behind me and spreads out across the two seats with her knitting and a bag of snacks. For a second, I'm sure we've left someone behind and then I remember Mindy's dog Bella has gone to a special B & B where there will be lots of other pups to play with. Aunty Bindi found it on the internet – they have pooch ball pits and paddling pools! Bella is going to have a **fab** time.

A few minutes later, the roof rack is on and the

last of the luggage is secured. Aunty Bindi and Uncle Tony get on and sit in the back row. Mustaf waves from outside and we all wave back.

"Ready, family?" Dad turns to ask us.

"Yes!" we all shout back.

"**Ready**, navigator?" Dad asks Manny, giving him a nod.

"**Aye aye, captain**!" Manny beams.

"You do know we're not on a **ship**?" Mindy giggles, which sets Manny and Dad chuckling too.

And just like that, we're **off**. As the minibus pulls away, I see our reflection in the windows of the houses. Our big black minibus gleams in the early sunlight, heaving with a pile of bright pink luggage on top. I hope Mustaf secured it all properly.

Aunty Bindi tries to get a **sing-song** going. I watch my street go by as we move down the road. Granny starts passing around snacks, savoury and sweet.

My tummy does a little **flip** as we head out of Birmingham and towards the motorway. This is it – no turning back now. Just for once, I hope this trip goes to plan!

watch. It's **8.06 a.m.** My tummy grumbles. I barely had any time for breakfast this morning, but luckily Granny Jas has brought a super big batch of her delicious **parathas**. Milo, Mindy and I happily share one of Granny's still-warm, foil-wrapped parcels as Dad drives us over hills and through countryside. We pass fields full of sheep and goats and horses. We even see some wind turbines – we've been learning about those in school.

While we eat, Mindy chats excitedly with Milo about the famous jewel, looking up more information on her phone.

"You know, Milo, this diamond is worth **three million pounds**! What would you do if you had that much money?"

"Could you buy a mansion?" Milo asks.

"Yeah, a nice one with a pool!" says Mindy. "Apparently, this **diamond** used to be owned by that film star – you know, the one who got married, like, eight times."

Milo nods like he knows who she means, but he actually looks confused. "Why are you so into diamonds all of a sudden?" he asks her.

"I got a gemstone kit for my birthday last year with loads of interesting facts in it. Did you know diamonds take **millions** of years to form and it takes a **load** of **heat** and **pressure**? It's really **amazing**!" Mindy enthuses.

Milo frowns. "Pressure? Like they're stressed

out by exams or something?"

Mindy snorts. "Oh, Milo, you are **funny**. Not that kind of pressure. Look, I'll show you this great article I found online."

Mindy scrolls on her phone and Milo thinks for a moment.

"I know what I'd do with three million pounds!" he says excitedly. "I'd build an **animal sanctuary**!"

Mindy shakes her head. "You really would, wouldn't you! That sounds like an **awesome** idea, Milo."

I smile at them getting on so well. I gaze out of the window. This country lane seems to be going on for ever. We should be nearly there soon, shouldn't we?

Dad must be feeling the same too. He rubs the back of his neck. "Manny, just check the satnav, will you? I could do with a rest stop. Too many cups of Granny's chai this morning. Can you find out where the nearest service station is?"

Manny reaches forward and presses some buttons on the satnav, which is set into the dashboard. The screen lights up and Manny keeps tapping away, but the satnav doesn't seem to be doing what he wants.

"Uncle, it's **not working**," he complains.

"It will work, **beta**, just switch it off and then back on again. That always works with my laptop anyway," Dad offers.

So Manny does as he's told and presses the off button. He gives it a second and then switches it back on again. The screen flickers back to life and a voice says, "**Hola, ¿a qué dirección quieres ir**?"

Manny looks confused and frowns. "**Huh**?"

"Press that red button," suggests Mum helpfully.

"No, never press the red button. Don't you ever watch the movies, Aunty?" exclaims Mindy.

"Oh, well, how about that blue button?" asks Mum.

"Hmm, looks harmless enough." Mindy shrugs. "Try it, bro."

Manny cautiously presses the blue button. The satnav responds: "**La distancia a Barcelona es de mil seiscientos noventa y dos kilómetros.**"

"Did it just say **Barcelona**? I can't be travelling to Barcelona, I've got far too much to do!" Granny Jas exclaims.

"I'm sure it's just an error." Mum looks back, smiling **nervously**.

"Stop messing around, Manny. Just put in the postcode I gave you. That should sort it out," Dad says. I can see him frowning in the rear-view mirror.

Milo leans over, grinning, and whispers, "Neesh, are your family trips always like this?"

"Yes," I whisper back.

"You're so lucky! Mine are always boring. Just me and Mum and sometimes my gran, but she just sleeps all the way. This is so much fun!" Milo beams and I know he really means it.

Meanwhile Manny is still fiddling with the satnav as it randomly throws out Spanish phrases.

"**Hola, ¿cómo estás**?"

"**¡Adiós, amigos**!"

"**¿Qué pasa**?"

30

"**Muy bien**."

"Ooh, Spanish is so romantic, we should learn,"
Aunty Bindi coos at Uncle Tony.

"Make it stop!" Mindy covers her ears.

"I'm trying!" an exasperated Manny shouts.

"Oh, Bhagavan! Let me see this high-tech
nonsense," says Granny, getting up out of her seat
and walking down the centre of the minibus to the
front.

"Mum, sit down! You can't walk about while I'm
driving," says Dad.

"I am your mother,
don't tell me what to
do," says Granny,
all matter-of-
fact, and she
gives the satnav
screen a good
whack with
her tiny fist.

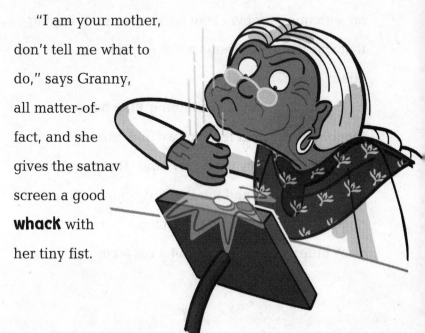

She's definitely broken it, I think to myself. But to our surprise the satnav screen blinks for a second and then comes back to life.

"**Please enter your destination**," says the satnav.

"There, see." Granny nods and returns to her seat.

"Just put the postcode in, Manny, **beta**, and we'll keep an eye out for the services. I don't think we should mess with that satnav any more," says Dad.

Manny dutifully enters the postcode and we carry on with our journey. I lean back in my seat, hoping that was the worst drama we're going to have on this family break.

It isn't long before something **else** happens though. At the next left turn we find ourselves on another quiet narrow country lane. There's not much space either side and the minibus scrapes against hedges and overhanging branches.

A little way ahead we spot a car facing us. It's a

muddy brown jeep. The mud is caked on so badly you can't even read the number plate.

"Oh dear, that car needs a good clean!" Aunty Bindi exclaims.

"It really does!" Manny says, turning round to face us. "Me and Mustaf could have that clean in no time. Mustaf has this polisher tool that makes the car so shiny!"

Uncle Tony laughs. "I'm glad you've been helping out, son, but how about you put that kind of dedication into tidying your room once in a while!"

The car is blocking the road so Dad waits a minute, but it soon becomes clear that the jeep isn't going to move. Dad manages to **squeeze** past slowly and we see there's a family inside, a bit like ours. There's a man, two teenage girls and an older woman wearing a green-and-pink patterned chunni like my Granny Jas. Dad tries to give them a wave but they don't look up. They're too busy staring at a map, probably figuring out directions.

We keep going and soon we're back on a main road, whizzing along. I settle back in my seat again and think about all the cool stuff we're going to see at the Space Centre in a couple of days.

We've been driving for about an **hour** when Mum says to Dad, "Darling, how much **further** do you think? We should be near Leicester now, shouldn't we?"

"Actually, yes. Manny, will you check the satnav, please? I still need the bathroom and we should have seen a service station by now," Dad says.

Manny leans forward and presses a button on the satnav. The computer voice says, "**Your destination is one hour and eighteen minutes away. You are on the fastest route**."

"That can't be right," says Dad. "Here, let me find somewhere to pull over so I can look at it properly."

"I don't trust all this **new-fangled** technology," mutters Granny.

"It can be really helpful, Granny. Look, I can get the map app up on my phone too," explains Mindy, holding her screen up for Granny to see.

"How does it know where we are all the time? They're **watching** us, I tell you!" she says knowingly.

"It's just satellites, Granny," I say. "They're really useful. A lot of everyday stuff relies on satellites millions of miles away in space. Don't you think that's **amazing**?"

"Pah! You won't say that when they're tracking you down. I watch those conspiracy films with your father. I know what goes on!" Granny wags her finger at me.

"What was the postcode again?" Mindy calls out, getting ready to tap it into her phone.

"Um, hang on. Let me check on the satnav. Okay, it's **LL55 4NY**," replies Manny.

"**LL?** Are you sure? According to the maps app on my phone, that postcode takes us to Mount Snowdon in **WALES**," Mindy says worriedly.

"Oh, that can't be right. Maybe it was **LE** not **LL**. I might have pressed the L twice by accident. Oops, sorry," says Manny as he realizes what he's done.

"**MANNY**!" everyone exclaims at the same time.

CHAPTER THREE

SUSPICION AT THE SERVICE STATION

"**Don't panic**, we'll just go back the other way!" says Dad brightly. "These things happen, **beta**, don't feel too bad. I'll turn around now. We'll be there in no time."

Manny smiles sheepishly and puts in the right postcode. The satnav says, "**You will reach your destination in one hour and fifty-seven minutes. There is traffic on your route**."

I slump back in my seat. This journey is turning into a **NIGHTMARE**. We should have just got the train.

"Um...I don't mean to be a pain, but I kind of

need the bathroom
now, too," Milo
says.

Manny looks
back at him
gratefully. "Me too!"

"I guess I could go too,
if we're stopping anyway,"
Mindy adds.

"Ah yes, I can stretch my
legs. These joints get stiff if I
sit too long," says Granny.

Bindi pipes up too. "Ooh,
can we see if they have any
magazines?"

"Okay, okay, everyone, I'll find a service station.
There should be one along the motorway. We're
getting back on it in a few minutes so try and **hold
on** till then, okay?" Dad says.

"Okay," Milo answers uncertainly.

☆ ✧ ★ ✩

A few miles later Milo is **jiggling** around in his seat
as we pull into the busy service station. Everyone
piles out of the minibus and we split into two groups.
Me, Dad and Aunty Bindi go to the shop to get
sweets and magazines. Everyone else except
Granny goes to find the toilets. She walks around
on the grass verge outside the service station,
exercising her joints the way the doctor showed her,
with stretches and bends. She's getting some
odd stares from people passing her, but she doesn't
care. I love that about Granny – she's always just
Granny.

I look at the books in the shop while Dad goes to
find "**a good old-fashioned A-Z**". Apparently,
that's what they used to call a book of maps. I don't
think he trusts the state-of-the-art satnav any more,
even though technically it was Manny who put in
the wrong postcode.

Aunty Bindi browses through the fashion

magazine section, **squealing** when she sees something she likes.

Dad and I go to the tills to pay. The queue is small, with only a few people ahead of us but the person at the till seems to be taking ages. There's a family just in front of us also waiting – a man, two teenagers and a woman wearing the exact same salwar kameez as my Granny Jas! They do look a bit familiar actually. And then I realize – it's that family from the muddy car in the lane! How funny! Dad recognizes them too.

"Oh, **hello**, I think we passed you on the way here. You were parked on that narrow road and we were in the oversized minibus squeezing past." Dad chuckles.

The other dad turns around, **startled**. "Oh, erm, hello." He's got light brown hair and a moustache that seems too big for his face. His sleeves on his jacket are rolled up and I see a glimpse of a line of tattooed stars. He sees me looking and tugs his sleeve down. He seems **nervous** like he's got something to **hide**.

Dad doesn't notice anything **weird** and carries on chatting. "Well, as it happens, we were going in the wrong direction when we passed you earlier. We're just stopping for a quick break before we head on to Leicester."

The man smiles tightly but doesn't reply. Dad talks at him about the weather and how he's buying a good old map because you can't rely on technology. I look at the other members of the family. The granny who looks like my granny from the back is fiddling with her chunni nervously and doesn't turn to face us fully. One of the teenage girls is on her phone and the other one seems to be staring down at her feet like there's something really interesting down there.

"Hi," I say. "I'm Anisha."

She doesn't reply.

Dad speaks into the **stone-cold** silence. "Have you got far left to travel?"

The other dad clears his throat like he's trying to think of an answer. His daughters look at him and back to each other. I realize they *all* look a bit nervous.

"Um, not far. We are going to Leicester also," he answers awkwardly.

"Ah, lovely. Well, maybe we'll see you there," says Dad. "Where are you all staying? We should meet up and take in some of the festival together. We're always happy to meet other families." He smiles. Dad is always befriending strangers everywhere we go. **SO EMBARRASSING!**

"We will be very busy and not there for long," the other dad replies, not answering my dad's question at all.

Just then Bindi joins us in the queue, waving her magazine at us. "Look, they've got that band, the **Bollydreamers**, on the front of *Asiana* magazine. Did you know they're rumoured to be coming to the UK?"

She notices the two girls, who for some reason she thinks are cute. "Oh, look at you two! I **love** the **matching-outfit thing** you have going on. We've got twins – younger than you, I think, but they would never let me get them matching outfits. I keep telling them tartan is in fashion now, but they won't listen." She pauses for breath. "I'm Bindi, by the way. We're the **Mistry** family – although now I'm married, I'm a Singh, but, you know, I still **feel** like a Mistry. What are your names?

You know, you look ever so **familiar**... Do I know you from somewhere?"

They both take a step back as she makes a fuss over them, and the dad stares at Aunty Bindi. "No, you **don't**, and they're not twins," he answers abruptly. "We are the **Patels**." Then he looks away as if to put an end to the conversation.

Dad interjects. "Bindi, you probably recognize them because we passed them on the road earlier."

"Oh, okay," Bindi says, seeming **surprised** at the Patels refusing to chat.

Luckily the till operator calls out, "Next, please," and the Patel family pay for their stuff, then disappear out of the shop.

Aunty Bindi shouts out "Goodbye!" as they leave, but they don't turn back.

"They were a little **rude**," she sniffs. "I was only trying to be **friendly**. Some people! Anyway, Anni, look at this band in my magazine. We should definitely go and see them if they do come to the UK. You'd love them."

I glance at the magazine, but Aunty Bindi is waving it about in front of my face because she's so **overexcited**, so I still don't know who she's talking about.

While Aunty Bindi witters on as she normally does, we head out of the shop and walk past a row of payphones. Who uses those any more? Hasn't everyone got mobile phones? I see **someone** is using one of them though...

It's Mr Patel, the dad from the other family! He doesn't see me and, as we pass by, I hear him say to whoever he's talking to, "Don't worry, we haven't been recognized. The disguise you suggested works a **treat**. This **wig** itches though and I have to keep gluing my **moustache** back on!" He rubs his hairline behind his ear and then he slides his finger underneath and I realize it is actually a wig! His real hair peeking out is a much

46

darker brown. He continues his conversation. "No one **suspects** a thing… No, my mobile phone is off – it's better that way in case anyone realizes I've left **America** already… Yes, we'll be there soon. No, no **police,** we don't need them interfering. Okay, I'll call when we get there."

I can hardly believe my ears. Is he some sort of **criminal**? I spot Milo outside the toilets and walk quickly to catch up with him.

"You'll never believe what I just heard!" I say, looking around to make sure no one's listening.

"What, Neesh? You've gone a **funny** colour. Are you okay?"

I lower my voice. "We just bumped into that family that we passed on the roadside a while back, remember? Anyway, they were a bit jumpy when my dad was talking to them in the shop and then, just now, I **overheard** the dad of that family on a **very** strange phone call. He was talking about not wanting anyone to know he'd left America and not wanting any police involved. **AND** he's wearing a **wig** and a **glued-on moustache**!"

"Okay, steady on, **Sherlock**," laughs Milo. "Firstly, people wear wigs for all kinds of reasons. And maybe he likes having a moustache but can't grow one. Secondly, it's pretty loud in here with people walking past all the time – are you sure that's what he said? Maybe you **misheard**? They're probably just a family on a road trip like us. Come on, this is our half-term and we're on holiday! Time to **chillax!**"

I sigh. He's right, it is noisy and the dad's voice *was* a bit muffled. Could I have **misheard**? Maybe he said "**please**" and not "**police**". We have been up since very early this morning, and I am tired. I could be mistaken. Besides what could I do even if they were up to no good?

We all walk out of the service station into the sunshine and towards our minibus. As we approach it, the muddy brown four-by-four goes past, and I can see the Patels inside.

Suddenly a BBC News van pulls into the car park just ahead of them, and for a second I think I see panic on their faces. The granny looks at the dad, **worried**. But the van drives past them and over to the entrance of the service station. The dad's shoulders relax and he smiles at the granny...but then he sees me watching and frowns. They drive away **very** quickly.

I don't say anything to Milo but I get a really **weird** feeling, like all this means something **not very good** is going to happen on this trip. But I'm probably getting carried away, right? Just because they were acting suspiciously and the dad was having a definitely dodgy phone call **AND** wearing a wig, that doesn't mean trouble, does it?

STRANGE FAMILY

+

DODGY DISGUISES

=

GUARANTEED TROUBLE!

Welcome to
LEICESTER
Historic City

CHAPTER FOUR

LEICESTER, AT LAST!

The rest of the journey goes smoothly and quietly and actually quite quickly. Aunty Bindi and Uncle Tony fall asleep side by side, heads back and mouths wide open. Granny Jas catches up on her knitting. She's making Dad a jumper out of bright orange wool. I don't know where he'll ever wear it. Mum and Dad chat away as he drives and Manny is on his tablet as usual. I put my **suspicions** about that Patel family and the phone call to the back of my mind while Mindy, Milo and I talk about what we're going to do when we get there.

Soon we see signs for Leicester and everyone starts to get excited. I check my watch. It's

11.23 a.m. now. It's taken us four hours to get here. I'm **so** tired!

Dad drives to the bed and breakfast place we are staying in, which is just round the corner from what they call the **Golden Mile** in Leicester. It's basically a **really** long road with all Indian shops along it. Food, clothes, spices, ornaments, jewellery – you name it, the Golden Mile has it. But today some of the roads around it are closed off for the festival and there are big banners everywhere advertising the performances, a fashion show and the jewellery exhibition. We can hear the **pounding** of **dhol drums*** as we get nearer and **Bollywood** music comes in waves through the open windows of the minibus. We all peer out, hoping to catch a glimpse of the crowds.

We have to drive round the narrow back streets a couple of times to find a parking space big enough

* Dhol drums are double-sided drums that look like a barrel. You wear them on a strap around your neck. Manny tried to learn them for a bit and Uncle Tony said Manny was the only person he knew that could play the drums out of tune!

to fit our minibus. Mum suggests paying for a car park even though she knows Dad won't. Eventually a couple of cars leave and there's enough room for our sixteen-seater to **squeeze** in. Uncle Tony gets out and guides Dad into the space. I do worry for a second that we're going to end up in someone's **living room** when Dad misjudges the amount of space he has to reverse into and we mount the kerb – but it's all okay in the end.

With a huge sigh of **relief**, we all get off the minibus and take in our surroundings. This street is made up of identical-looking houses all connected, one joined to the next joined to the next and so on to the end of the road, apart from a gap about halfway down.

"We don't have to unload everything now, do we?" Manny asks **cautiously**.

"No, we'll deal with that later. It might take a while and I need a cup of chai first," jokes Dad. "Let's all go to the B & B to freshen up, then we can head out and see some of the festival before lunch. Does that sound okay to everyone? I've got my booking confirmation – it says the B & B is just down here."

There's a bit of **grumbling** but we follow Dad in single file down the street. He takes an abrupt turn where there is a gap between two of the houses, down an alleyway.

"Are you sure it's this way, darling?" asks Mum.

"Yes, I think so. Mum, you said Mrs Kumar told you about this place, didn't she?" Dad calls back to Granny Jas.

"Heh? I can't hear you properly from back here," Granny Jas shouts.

"He said, Mrs Kumar told you about this B & B, didn't she?" Milo shouts in Granny's ear.

"Ah, no need to shout, Milo, **beta**!" Granny yelps, holding her ears.

Just then, Dad stops up ahead at a doorway in the side of a building. Above the faded brown door is a sign that says **SHSG B & B**. I wonder what it means.

"I think this is it," Dad says
doubtfully. "It doesn't look like
much of a B & B though."

"Don't judge a book by its cover,"
Granny insists and pushes past us all,

54

almost knocking me sideways. "Come on, no time to waste." She grins and opens the door.

We step into a dimly lit reception. It's quite big inside, actually. In front of us there is a high desk with a lamp on it and a bell. A ceiling fan whirs round and round above our heads and the hum of a vacuum comes from somewhere in the building. Dad hits the bell with his hand and smiles at us all nervously. We wait for what seems like ages. Suddenly a woman appears behind the desk out of the darkness beyond it. She looks a bit like Granny with a long plait, though her hair is black with silver-grey streaks running through it. On her forehead she wears a black tika* dot.

"Ah, you must be the Mistry family. I am Kangana, the owner of this humble establishment. I've been expecting you."

* A tika is also known as a bindi. It's a black or red dot that is worn by Hindu people for religious reasons. Bindis can also be worn for decoration and can be sequinned and colourful. My Aunty Bindi, who obviously shares her name with the bindi, loves them and she says the bigger they are, the better!

"Oh, you have?" Dad asks uncertainly.

She laughs. "Yes, **silly**, we have a record of everyone who has booked online to stay with us."

"Ah yes, of course," Dad replies. "Well, I'm Pavan Mistry, this is my wife Bhavana, my daughter Anni and her friend Milo, my sister-in-law Bindi and her husband Tony, their two children Mindy and Manny and, last but definitely not least, my mother. We are rather a **large** group."

Kangana nods. "Don't you worry about that, we've got plenty of room. It's so very lovely to meet you all. Has anyone got any questions about the facilities before I show you to your rooms?"

"Have you got Wi-Fi here?" Milo asks, fiddling with his cap-cam.

"It looks a bit small, are you sure you have enough rooms? Have we got our own beds? I'm not sharing with him." Mindy points to her brother.

"What kind of breakfast do we get?" asks Manny, ignoring his sister.

"Yeah, that's a better question than mine, answer his first," agrees Milo.

Kangana raises her hand. "Ha, very **inquisitive** minds, I see, and all good questions. I will try to answer them as we go. But don't worry about space, we have plenty. We are not quite what we seem from the outside." She winks. "Come along now. I'm afraid there are a few stairs though and we don't have a lift."

So we all follow Kangana up the stairs. Aunty Bindi chats excitedly to her, asking about the nearest shops and the fashion show at the festival. We climb two flights of stairs to the top of the B & B to find a surprisingly wide hallway with four rooms opposite each other.

"Here you go, a family room with an adjoining single room as you requested and two double rooms," Kangana says.

"Can us kids stay together?" Manny asks. "My dad **snores**! Plus, I'd rather be with Milo and Anisha."

Mindy hard-stares at him.

Manny sighs. "And my sister, I suppose!"

Mum laughs. "Yes, I suppose that would be okay. The rooms are close together and you can have the big one with the attached single room so Granny Jas can keep an eye on you all."

Kangana hands the room keys to Mum. "I'll leave you to settle in. Perhaps I can answer the rest of the children's questions downstairs when you're ready? If you need me at any time during your stay, you know where I am."

As soon as Kangana leaves, Milo and Manny run through the open door of the family room and jump on the beds, shouting, "**Woohoo**, holidays!"

Mindy and I look at each other and then turn to Mum. "Do we have to share with them?" we both say.

CHAPTER FIVE

THE FESTIVAL

After everyone has chosen (**fought over**) which bed they're sleeping in tonight and Mindy has made sure she is definitely not sharing a bed with Manny, we head back downstairs. Kangana is nowhere to be seen, so I guess our questions will have to wait till later. We leave the lobby and step back out into the sunlight. I have to blink a few times before my eyes adjust. Almost immediately everyone starts talking at once. Aunty Bindi and Uncle Tony want to go clothes shopping and then for lunch at the Bollywood-themed restaurant they've read about. Mum wants to visit the festival market and she's dragging Dad with her. Granny Jas says she wants to get her spices.

Mindy, Manny, Milo and I want to go and explore.

"I'm not sure I like the idea of you kids wandering off without one of us with you. Wouldn't you like to come to the market with us, Anni?" Mum asks.

"No, Mum! We're not babies, plus there are four of us. **Safety in numbers**, right? And the twins have their phones if we need you. Also, it's the Golden Mile – as in, it's one straight road. We can't get lost," I reason. I feel Milo, Mindy and Manny gather behind me in agreement.

Mum laughs, retreating. "Okay, okay, you've persuaded me. But share your location with your father, Manny. I'm sure that's a thing, isn't it?" she asks.

"I'm impressed, Aunty. Yes, I can share my phone location with Dad. We do it all the time. He likes to know where we are too," Manny says, grinning at Uncle Tony.

"Ha, yes. **Someone** has to worry about what you're getting up to," Uncle Tony replies, handing Manny some money for snacks.

After Dad lectures us on how to cross the road, why we shouldn't speak to strangers and how to find north if we get lost**(!?)** we finally get away from all the grown-ups. For the first time since we left our house, I start to feel **relaxed**.

We head onto Belgrave Road, the Golden Mile. It's been totally blocked off from traffic so everyone can just walk in the road. The whole area is **heaving** with people and we have to weave our way through the crowds.

Milo clicks on his cap-cam. "I don't want to miss any of this! Mum was gutted she couldn't come with us. She's working this weekend but I said I'd **record** everything so she can see it when we get back," he says with a smile.

"I wonder what there is to see," I say. "We could do with a map of the festival."

"That woman looks like she works here, maybe she'll have a map?" suggests Manny, pointing.

We look across the road to see a woman holding a clipboard and wearing a headset with earphones so **big** it looks like she's an air traffic controller or about to fly a helicopter!

"Excuse me, do you work here?" I ask, moving closer, not sure if she can hear me.

The woman looks towards me and smiles. She lifts the headset off her ears and rests it round her neck like a travel pillow, revealing big **sparkly** earrings.

"Hello there. Yes, actually I'm the organizer here. Everything you see, the whole festival, was organized by me," she says proudly.

"**Wow**, you've done a great job!" I say, looking around, impressed.

"Thank you, that's so nice of you to say. I'm Bhoomi." She holds out her hand. "Bhoomi Biddum. We're very excited to have such a great theme this year. '**Wonders of the World**' and the diamond display has attracted a lot of publicity." She grins.

"Those earrings are pretty," Mindy comments.
"Our stepmum **loves** sparkly things."

"Ah, these old things? Just costume jewellery –
I love my trinkets." Bhoomi smiles, fiddling with an
oversized earring. "Now, what are you children most
looking forward to at the festival? We have so
much on offer. Let me give you a map of all
the stands." She pulls a leaflet from her
clipboard and gives it to me.

"Thank you," I say.

"Are you here with
family?" Bhoomi
enquires.

"Yes, these are
my cousins Mindy
and Manny and
this is my friend
Milo. We've got my
granny and parents

and aunty and uncle with us too, but they're all off shopping and we wanted to explore," I answer.

"Ah yes, you young people **SHOULD** be off exploring. I wish I could join you!" She looks at her watch. "Anyway, I must dash, I have to be somewhere. Enjoy the festival, **darlings**!" And she blows us a kiss as she hurries away, putting the great big headset back on.

She's wearing red velvet boots with glinting silver heels that clack loudly on the pavement. The toes of the boots are pointed and jewel-encrusted. The light bounces off them as she walks.

Aunty Bindi would like those too, I think to myself.

"She was friendly," says Milo.

"Look, there's a sign for the jewellery exhibition, can we go in there first?" Mindy asks **excitedly**, pointing across the road.

"Yeah, let's go see this **famous diamond** Mindy's so excited about. Get it over with. I bet it's not even that **big**," Manny says, nudging her. Mindy nudges him back and sticks her tongue out.

We follow the signs, which lead us further up the road. The jewellery exhibition is being held inside the Leicester Museum and Art Gallery. It's an old building with tall columns at the front. Above the entrance is a huge banner that reads

Leicester Museum

World-Famous Diamond on Display Here!

Out front is a display board with lots of facts about the museum on it. Milo stops to read.

"Leicester Museum and Art Gallery has been bringing people together to enjoy art, history and science for over **170 years**."

"Wow, that's a long time! Imagine all the people who have walked through those doors!" Manny remarks.

I read the next one. "In the 1930s, Leicester Museum and Art Gallery inspired local boy **David Attenborough** to explore his love of the natural world. **Wow**, Milo, your idol, David Attenborough, came here!" I say, impressed.

Milo gawps. "No way! Now I definitely want to go inside!"

It's free to enter and surprisingly there's not much of a queue, so we walk in through the huge doors. There are a few people milling about looking at exhibits, but it's pretty quiet. The first room has lots of old paintings in it by famous artists. We pass

through that one quickly. The next room is more interesting, with fossils including a **huge** T-Rex tooth. Milo is super excited about those, of course. I have to admit, it's pretty amazing to think that these huge creatures wandered the earth before us.

Next, we move into the third room, the one Mindy is most excited about: the jewellery exhibit. Just by the door there is a security guard sitting on a chair. He's busy playing on his phone – sounds like a racing game. We walk past him and the banners that say **World-Famous Diamond**.

Straight away we see it. The diamond **glistens** in the light and for once we all fall silent. It's about the size of a small potato or a ping-pong ball, which doesn't sound that big, but trust me, for a diamond, it's **massive**! It's flat on the top and comes to a sharp point at the bottom. It's resting on a purple velvet cushion under a glass dome.

Milo whistles, Manny gawps and I suck in a breath.

"See, I told you! It's pretty impressive, right?" Mindy says.

I look around the semicircular room. The lighting is dimmer in here, with spotlights hanging down from the ceiling. There are a few cases of smaller jewels dotted along the edge, but the main attraction is in the centre, in a glass domed case on top of a stand. We crowd around it to get a better look.

"Imagine owning that!" Milo says. "I could buy my mum the biggest house ever and she'd never have to work again!"

"The only way one of us is ever going to own something like that is by stealing it," I say, "and that would be a pretty daft thing to attempt."

"I'd make a great **cat burglar** – you know, those guys who sneak in and sneak out without being seen. I'm good at stealth missions," says Milo, crouching down to demonstrate.

"I bet they have **alarms** all over this place," Mindy says. "They probably have those red laser beams you see on telly, too! Look, there's a camera up there." She points.

"Plus, we're not jewel thieves, or **anything-thieves** for that matter," adds Manny.

"Alright, alright," laughs Milo. "I can dream, can't I? I still think I'm **stealthy**," he says, as he accidentally knocks into a wooden gem case behind him.

I chuckle. "Let's go, Milo, before you get us all into trouble."

We head back out of the room the way we came, passing the security guard, who is still on his phone. We pop to the gift shop and Milo buys a replica diamond on a key ring for his mum. "She'll love this!" He grins.

"Imagine if you took her the real one!" laughs Mindy.

"Nah, I've decided, I don't think I want to be a diamond thief after all," Milo replies. "If they put Anisha on the case, I'd be caught in about five minutes!"

CHAPTER SIX

HUNGRY DOGS AND BHANGRA DANCING

As we walk down the Golden Mile, the aroma of freshly cooked treats **wafts** around us. Outside one shop I can smell fried samosas and pakoras. We pass a restaurant and the whiff of hot chicken curry and tandoori fish makes my tummy **rumble**.

There are pop-up food stands as part of the festival. To tie in with the **Wonders of the World** theme, one stall has a model of the pyramids made up of different coloured mithai and gelebi. It's so tempting to stop and have something at every stand. In the end we pick up some hot samosas with the money that Uncle Tony gave Manny and we eat as we walk.

"I think you made a friend, Milo," laughs Mindy, nodding towards a scruffy-looking dog trailing behind us, lapping up the pastry crumbs Milo is dropping as he walks.

Milo turns and looks and stops in his tracks.

"**MILO, NO!**" I warn, but it's too late. Milo hugs the quite obviously stray dog and feeds it some more samosa.

"I don't think dogs are supposed to eat samosa, are they?" asks Manny.

"It's an Indian dog, obviously. Look, he loves it!" Milo smiles at the dog. "Don't you, boy?"

The dog licks his face.

"**Urgh**, Milo, you have no idea where that dog has been. He's probably got **fleas**!" I warn.

Milo covers the dog's big floppy ears. "Don't say that, he can hear you!"

"How do you know it's a boy dog? It could be a girl," Mindy challenges.

"Well, let's see, shall we?" Milo says, and sticks his head under the dog to look at its bottom end. The dog stands there looking slightly **alarmed**, but thankfully doesn't move – or worse, **wee** on Milo's head.

"**MILO**!" Mindy, Manny and I say all at once.

Milo rears his head back up again, looking only slightly embarrassed. "I think we can safely say he is a she. Well, I think she's lovely!"

"I think we should call her **Samosa**," says Manny. "She seems to love them."

We all laugh then and Milo breaks into a grin. "I like that. What do you think, Samosa?" The dog licks Milo's hand and wags her tail. Then she takes the last bit of his samosa and runs off.

"Come back, girl!" Milo shouts, but the dog

is gone. His shoulders sag sadly. "I thought we could be friends."

"I'm sorry, Milo. We could let animal rescue know and they can keep a lookout for her, but we'll never find her in this crowd now," I say, patting him on the arm.

"Okay, I guess. I just thought we had a connection. I know you all think I don't really have **animal intuition**, but I **do** feel something when I'm around animals and she was **special**."

"We might see her again," offers Mindy.

"Yeah, we'll all keep a lookout," adds Manny.

After Manny searches for the local dog rescue centre on his phone and calls them to tell them about Samosa, we keep walking. We see a stand with silk scarves and embroidered tunics in every colour imaginable. Further down there's a fashion show with models dressed up in dazzling outfits, sashaying along the catwalk that is connected to a circular stage. Upbeat Indian pop music blares from the speakers either side of the area. I think for a second that I see Granny, but when the woman turns around I realize it's not her.

Actually, now I'm looking, there sure are a lot of grannies here in Leicester. Maybe they're all here for the spices like my Granny Jas?

Milo cheers up a bit at the music. He nods his head and the cap-cam wobbles about.

Pag (turban)

Torla (fan-shaped bit)

Kaintha (necklace)

Milo (obv)

Kurta (long shirt)

We walk along a bit further and see **bhangra dancers**. They're wearing traditional dress: baggy trousers with a sash at the waist, loose-fitting long colourful shirts and turbans with matching silk fans on the front. They pull Milo up to have a go with them and he's quite good actually! They all bend their knees and kick out their feet, pumping their arms in the air in perfect sync above their heads. Milo is clearly **loving** it.

Lungi
(Sash)

Jugi
(waistcoat)

Mindy and Manny get distracted and wander into a shop that has loads of colourful and festive decorations in the window, so I stand to the side and wait. I like **people-watching**, wondering what kind of lives they lead and what kind of day they're having. **Ooh**, is that **Granny**? Oh no, this lady has a blue headscarf, and Granny's is green with a pink pattern.

I spot one child with a huge balloon and another with a big bag of sweets. Two more grannies chatting on a bench. A man with a big beard, who's carrying a tiny little dog. There's **another** elderly woman who looks a bit like Granny! Weird how some strangers look so familiar.

WAIT! There's a face I really do recognize. That's the dad from the **Patel** family! He sees me and recognizes me too. He looks surprised, then he looks from side to side and scratches under his wig nervously, before stepping back and disappearing into the crowd.

79

I try to get Milo's attention to tell him, but he's being lifted onto the shoulders of the bhangra dancers and not looking this way at all. Suddenly I'm distracted by shouting.

"No, **no**, put him **down**! Health and safety! No members of the public to be involved in acrobatics. We are not insured for that!"

A man wearing a purple jacket and a huge headset like the one Bhoomi Biddum had on **yells** at Milo and the bhangra dancers. He's carrying a clipboard too with the name **Parvesh** in large lettering

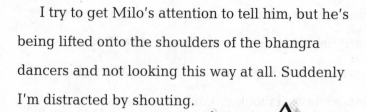

80

on the back. The dancers stop what they're doing and gently place Milo on the ground, while Parvesh waves the clipboard at them.

Milo runs over to me. "That was so much fun! I don't know what his problem is."

The man comes **marching** this way. "The **problem**, dear boy, is that you could break your neck and then who will everyone **blame**?" he says. "**Me**, that's who, the assistant. And worse than that, **SHE'LL** be furious and that will be my career over!" And with that, he stomps away.

Milo and I just look at each other. But before we have a chance to say anything, there's another **kerfuffle** behind us and the crowd seems to part.

"Neesh, **look**!" Milo points.

I glance round and see a policeman and -woman running right towards us! I grab Milo's arm and pull him out of the way as they hurry past and down the road. We push through the crowd to see what's going on. Two minutes later we're in front of the big

columns at the Museum and Art Gallery again.
There's an alarm blaring from within the building and
I get that feeling in my tummy that I always get when
something bad happens. We stand over to the side by
a bench.

The security guard comes out looking very **pale**
and staggers over to sit down.

"Are you okay?" I ask.

"It's just not **possible**," he says, shaking his head.

"What's not **possible**?" Milo asks.

"I just don't understand it," the guard mutters
more to himself than anyone. "The box was alarmed
and we have CCTV. I only stepped away for a
minute…well, maybe **five**. I don't understand how
they could have **stolen** it in **broad daylight** and
hidden it so quickly."

"**Stolen what?**" Milo and I ask together, even
though I think I already know.

The security guard looks at us. He gulps and then
says, "The diamond. It's been **STOLEN**!"

CHAPTER SEVEN

ACCUSED!

Before the guard can tell us anything else about the diamond being **stolen**, he gets called back into the museum. The crowd gets **bigger** and people **push** and **shove** as more police officers arrive. Sirens **wail** and the festival-goers part for arriving squad cars, which block the road either side of the entrance to the exhibition. Those standing nearby whisper and nudge each other. Nobody can quite **believe** it. The world-famous diamond – **STOLEN**!

A man begins to cordon off the entrance to the exhibition with official police tape, ordering everyone in the crowd to move backwards. Mindy and Manny find us in the herd of people somehow.

Leicester Museum

World-Famou
Diamond on
Display Here!

More police officers are arriving by the minute. Two more squad cars pull up with their lights **flashing** and a very **serious-looking** woman with short brown hair gets out of one of them. She's not in a police uniform like the other officers – she's wearing a long black coat, a crisp white shirt and smart black trousers.

"I bet she's a **detective,**" whispers Milo.

The officers step out of the woman's way as she approaches the entrance to the exhibition. She stops for a second and scans the crowd as if she's looking for someone. Her gaze stops on us. I smile **nervously** even though I haven't done anything wrong.

Oh no! Maybe she'll think I've got something to hide because I'm smiling. I change my face to a frown, which probably looks really strange now. Milo nudges me as if to say **Stop being weird**.

The woman raises an eyebrow, whispers something to one of the officers nearby and strides into the exhibition.

"That was **intense**!" says Milo.

"This is so **cool**! Look at the crowd. Do you think they'll find a real criminal?" Manny wonders out loud.

Mindy shakes her head. "Don't be silly, Manny, this isn't a police show off the telly. And what criminal would be so daft as to stick around long enough to be arrested!"

Suddenly there are murmurs as the detective emerges from the museum. She's followed by several officers.

"Clear a path, we're bringing her out!" an officer yells.

"Her?" Manny says. "It's a woman thief?"

"Women can be **baddies** too, Manny," says Mindy raising one eyebrow at him.

I wait, holding my breath. A **real-life** criminal.

A real heist, right here in Leicester. Who would try to steal a world-famous diamond in broad daylight and in the middle of a busy festival?

I try to picture what this thief might look like. I imagine a woman in a catsuit and balaclava, with a utility belt for all her jewel-stealing tools.

Just then there is more commotion at the entrance. The person being marched out is **not** a cat burglar and doesn't look anything like I expected.

Because in my wildest dreams I would never have imagined that it would be **OUR GRANNY JAS** being marched out of the exhibition by two police officers!

But it *is* her!

There must be some **mistake**!

I leap forward. "Granny!"

"Move along, young lady. This is a crime scene now." A stern officer holds me back.

"But that's her granny!" Milo insists, trying to step forward too.

"I said, move along." The policewoman clearly means business.

Granny spots us in the crowd and calls out.

"Don't worry, **beta**, this is all a silly misunderstanding. Will you get your dad for me? He will tell them." She glares up at one of the officers. "My son is a **lawyer** – he'll eat you for breakfast with a nice cup of **chai**. And will you stop pulling me! If I trip and fall I will **sue**! I know my **rights**! I watch these legal eagle programmes!"

"Just come along, madam. You were caught **red-handed** holding the glass box that had been protecting the jewel. It would be better for everyone if you tell us what you've done with the diamond." The detective sighs.

My stomach churns. That can't be true! How **ridiculous**! But then...Granny was supposed to be off buying spices. What on earth was she doing in the museum anyway? This is so **confusing**!

"I was putting the glass box back! The elaram was going off and I thought the glass case had been knocked off. I was just trying to help!" Granny answers the detective matter-of-factly.

"**Elaram**? What's that then?" One of the officers smirks.

"She means alarm, it's just how she says it. There's no need to make fun of her," I shout.

There's a murmur of approval in the crowd and

a voice further back yells, "Let her go! She's just someone's granny!"

Someone else calls out, "Yeah, go and catch a **real** criminal."

The officers and the detective look uncomfortable. "Just get her in the car, we'll question her properly at the station," the detective says. "Grab the CCTV footage from the building security and find out what the guard was doing instead of watching the diamond. I knew we should have insisted on having our own people looking after it. **Amateurs!**" she growls, glaring at the poor security guard, who is standing nearby, wringing his hands.

Just then I see a familiar face in the crowd and relief floods through me. **It's Dad!** Surely he'll be able to sort this out.

"We heard the commotion from down the road. What on earth is going on?" he exclaims, rushing over to us with Mum following closely behind.

"They are talking nonsense, **beta**!" Granny cries. "They think I stole that diamond! Can you imagine?" She shakes her head at the young officer, who goes bright red and looks away.

"This is **ridiculous**. What **evidence** do you have? You can't arrest an elderly lady for nothing. Come on, be reasonable," says Dad. "She's my mother. I'll vouch for her – I'm a lawyer."

"I'm sorry, sir, but the law is the law, as you well know. This woman…that is to say, your mother was found at the **scene of the crime**. At the very least she needs to answer some **serious** questions," the officer replies curtly. "We have to take her to the station. You can meet us there if you like," he adds more softly upon seeing Dad's anxious face.

"I'll sort this out, Mum, I promise," Dad vows as Granny Jas is escorted into a blue, yellow and white police car.

"I know you will, **beta**. I did not do this, and these **daft** people will soon realize that." Granny smiles but it's not her usual grin and I know deep down she's a bit **worried** too.

"I can't believe this is happening, Neesh." Milo sighs as Granny gets into the car.

"Me neither, Milo. But I know one thing for sure – my granny wouldn't steal. There is more to this and I'm going to find out the **truth**."

CHAPTER EIGHT

WHAT NOW?

As Granny is driven away, Aunty Bindi and Uncle Tony arrive. Aunty Bindi goes into **meltdown** of course. Uncle Tony tries to calm her. The crowd starts to disperse and soon it's only me and my family standing at the side of the road, wondering what on earth just happened. Bhoomi, the festival organizer from earlier, comes running over, her heels clicking on the pavement. She looks very **dishevelled** compared to when we saw her before. Her headset is hanging round her neck and she's even missing an earring.

"I just heard about the diamond – I can't **believe** it!" she says, all out of breath. "I was so looking forward to seeing it too. I haven't had a chance to visit the exhibition with how busy we've been. Someone mentioned they arrested the **thief** straight away though."

"Not a thief, **MY GRANNY**!" I snap.

"Oh..." Bhoomi steps back. "I'm so sorry, I didn't realize. Is there anything I can do? There's some mistake, I'm sure," she tries to reassure us.

Dad steps forward. "That's very kind of you – it's all just a very strange mix-up." He holds out his hand. "We haven't met. I'm Anisha's dad, Mr Mistry."

She takes it and says, "I'm Bhoomi. I'm in charge of the festival so, please, if there is anything I can do, let me know. I must go and check in with the security staff and find out what exactly has gone on, but here's my card. I'm around all weekend while the festival is on." She smiles, gives my arm a quick supportive squeeze and clicks away into the exhibition.

"Right, I suppose I should get down to the police station," Dad says, scratching his head.

"I'm coming too," I say firmly.

"I don't think that's a good idea, Anni. Let's just take a minute to think." Mum frowns.

"We should all go for moral support," Bindi says.

"That's an even worse idea!" Mum says.

"Why? Give me a second and I'll make a banner that says **Free Granny Jas!** We'll stage a sit-in till they let her go. I've always wanted to protest for a worthy cause," Bindi tells us excitedly.

"Um, I'm not sure that's necessary just yet, Aunty Bindi," I say cautiously. "I mean, I'm sure Granny would appreciate the support, but maybe let's wait and see what they say when we get there. I'm sure it's all been a big **misunderstanding** that'll be cleared up in no time, right, Dad?"

"Why don't we get everyone back to the B & B?" Uncle Tony suggests. "I missed lunchtime – let's order in some food." He nods at Mum and Dad. "You two go and check on Granny and make sure she's okay. You can find out what's going to happen and if Granny has to stay overnight."

"**STAY OVERNIGHT?**!" I shout, horrified.

"Yes, there's a possibility they might keep her in for questioning," Dad admits.

"But she doesn't know anything. I don't understand why this is happening," I sob.

"Look, they might just need to know if she saw anyone **lurking** about in there. She could have **valuable** information but not know it until they ask her the right questions. Let the police do their job and they'll soon realize Granny has **nothing** to do with all this. Besides, you know Granny Jas – she's very capable of looking after herself. She'll be running the police station soon, I'll bet!" Tony smiles.

"Okay, I guess," I say taking a deep breath and wiping my tears. Even though I just want Granny to come back right now, the image of her wearing a police uniform and telling everyone what to do does bring a small smile to my face. I have to stay positive and keep busy. And I know exactly *how* I'm going to keep busy.

"I'm not ready to go back to the B & B yet," I say.

"Well, we could hang out at the festival a bit longer..." Milo chips in, giving me a look that says he knows what I'm planning.

Uncle Tony looks at Aunty Bindi and sighs. "Well, okay, but all four of you stay together. I'm still tracking your phone, Manny, so no wandering off and definitely **no interfering** with the police investigation!" he warns. "I know you lot too well."

So in the end, Mum and Dad go to the police station and Uncle Tony and Aunty Bindi head back to the B & B, leaving the four of us behind: me, Milo, Mindy and Manny.

Milo turns to me. "Right, Neesh, what's the plan? How are we going to clear Granny's name?"

"Milo, your cap-cam – please tell me it was still recording when we were walking around?"

Milo reaches for the top of his head.

"Yeah, but actually, where **IS** my cap? It was on my head!"

Just then there's a **WOOF!** It's Samosa the dog! Milo runs over and leans down. "You came back, girl! Can you help me? Find my cap, Samosa; can you find it, girl?"

Samosa woofs again as if to say **YES!** She sniffs Milo's hand and then starts sniffing around on the ground.

"I hope she finds it. Mum will go mad if I've lost it," Milo worries. We all try to look but then Samosa comes running up with something between her teeth!

Milo pats her affectionately. "You found it! Where was it? Never mind, I'm just glad to have it back.

What a clever detective dog you are!"

"It probably got knocked off your head in the crowd just now," Mindy says.

"Milo, it's not **broken**, is it?" I ask.

"No, I don't think so," he says, checking it over.

"Good. Can we replay what's on it?"

"I think so," Milo replies. "I guess we could connect it to Manny's phone and replay it on there? I have the lead in my pocket."

"Great, let's find a quiet spot where we can sit down," I say.

There's a bench just behind us, so we perch there.

"Oh, I wish I had a pen and paper. I left my notebook in my overnight bag," I say.

Mindy does something really **lovely** then – something I could never have imagined a year ago. She hands me her **much-loved** notebook. "You can use mine if you like." She smiles.

"Thanks, that means a lot. I know how much you love your notebook," I say.

"It's for important stuff and this is **important**."

Mindy shrugs and hands me a pen.

I take a deep breath, opening the notebook at the next blank page. "**Okay**, so what do we know?"

CHAPTER NINE

GRANNY IN A GREEN CHUNNI

The four of us sit on the bench outside the museum. Milo sets up the cap-cam with Manny's phone so we can watch it. While we wait for them to do that I worry – what if the list of things we know is just one thing? The jewel was stolen and Granny Jas was arrested for it!

Thankfully, Mindy speaks up. "Well, we know the diamond was in its case when we went to the museum. What time was that?"

"Around twelve thirty?" I say, looking at my watch. "It's half past one now. So that means we have an hour window when the jewel was stolen."

"There was a camera in the room, wasn't there?" Manny remembers. "So won't that footage show the real thief? The police just need to check it."

"But I can't sit around here waiting for that – what if the camera went wrong or something? If there's even a small chance that we can prove Granny's innocence **AND** catch the real thief before the police sort this out, then we have to do it," I say.

Milo grins at me. "You normally don't like to be involved in any **drama,** Neesh."

"Well, this is **my granny** we're talking about. It's different," I say.

Mindy pats my hand. "She's **our** granny too. She looks after all of us, including Milo. We'll catch whoever did this, Anisha."

"I know," I say, even though my stomach feels like it's got a stone in it. I look back at the notepad. "So, we know when it happened and we know where. We just don't know who or how," I say.

"Maybe someone saw something when the

diamond was stolen?" Milo offers. "But how would we track down any witnesses?"

"Maybe **WE** saw something but didn't realize it was important earlier," I say.

"Okay, but Manny and I were in that shop at the time of theft, Milo was bhangra dancing and you were watching Milo. I'm not sure any of us saw anything useful," Mindy says.

I rack my brain and then it comes to me. I'd forgotten in all the kerfuffle. "I saw that **Patel** dad!" I blurt out. "That was weird. I'm sure he was wearing a **wig** and **fake moustache**. And when he noticed me looking at him, he disappeared into the crowd."

"Are you sure, Neesh? Why would he have anything to do with this?" Milo asks.

"Milo, I'm telling you he was acting **dodgy** at the service station and he was acting **dodgy** at the festival – I'm not making it up!" I say indignantly. "He was up to something."

Milo raises his hands in surrender. "Okay,

I believe you, Neesh. Let's see if we caught him on the cap-cam. There might be other stuff on there too. You can start making a list of people we need to investigate."

I harrumph but do as Milo suggests. I write down the word **SUSPECTS** and underline it. Then I write:

Patel dad (seen just before the theft at the festival)

Manny presses play and we all gather round his phone. We get to the bit where we went into the museum. On the film, the time in the bottom corner of the screen says **12.30**, so I jot this down in the notebook.

Milo's cap-cam has filmed us walking through all the exhibits and then finally through to the main room, where the jewel was all safe and sound in its case. We watch as we pass the security guard, busy on his phone.

"How did the thief get past him?" Manny asks.

"When the security guard ran out of the museum just before they arrested Granny Jas, he said he had left his post for a few minutes. So that must be when the thief saw their **opportunity** and stole the diamond," I deduce, quite pleased we are starting to pull a theory together already.

"I've got a question," says Mindy. "Where did they hide it? Did the thief just walk out of there with it?"

"Hey, do you think they might have **hidden** it somewhere nearby so they could come back for it later?" I ask.

"What if they hid it in this hedge?" Milo says. "Manny, help me look!" They both immediately start foraging around in the hedge behind the bench.

"I doubt it's in there," Mindy calls out, but they don't hear her. They're both on their hands and

knees, heads thrust into the branches.
Samosa joins in too and I can't help
but chuckle.

Mindy and I carry on watching the footage of us
leaving the museum via the main foyer.

"Mindy, **pause** it there," I say.

"What, here? It's just a bunch of people in the
entrance to the museum," she replies.

"Look at that woman. The one in the **green
chunni** with the **pink pattern** just like the one
Granny Jas was wearing."

"Is it Granny?" Mindy asks worried.

I look more closely. "No, it's definitely not Granny Jas."

"How can you be so sure?"

"She's too **tall** to be Granny. She's standing against the museum sign on the wall. Look, when I stand against it my head reaches the top of the sign."

"**Okaaay**," Mindy says, unsure where I'm going with this line of thought.

"**SO**," I say, "the woman on the film is at least a head and a half taller than the sign. **That's not Granny!**"

"How do you know. It's not like there's a measuring tape there!" Mindy points out.

"Well, it's not that **scientific** but if Granny Jas stood next to me in front of that sign, her head would be here," I say pointing to the wall. I know this because she always kisses the top of my head when she hugs me and the top of my head comes up to Granny Jas's **nose.** I shrug. "I just **know** that's not her."

Mindy looks at me, at the wall and back to the cap-cam footage. "I think you're **right**." She smiles.

I smile back, glad she gets it. "Okay, what else can we see on the footage? What does she have in her hands?" I say.

We both squint to try and see. "Is it some sort of **tool**?" Mindy asks.

"It's too hard to tell. It's like she's trying to hide it; it's tucked inside her fist," I say.

"It looks like pliers or some kind of **cutters** to me. I sometimes help Mustaf with jobs around the house – it's kind of fun." Mindy shrugs.

"*If* that's what they are, why on earth would anyone be carrying pliers or cutters into a museum?" I say.

"Because they were going to **steal** something!" Milo **shouts**, jumping up out of the hedge and almost knocking Manny over. Manny emerges covered in leaves and bits of stick.

Second on the suspect list, I write down, **Granny in green chunni**.

"How do we find her, though?" I say, looking around us. "She could be **anywhere** by now."

"The theft only happened, like, half an hour ago. She could still be in the area. It's worth a look around, right?" Milo reasons.

So once Milo and Manny have shaken off the last of the leaves and twigs, which Samosa thinks is a game of **fetch**, we leave the bench outside the museum and head down the main street back to the festival. There are still a few police officers around, but they don't seem to be on the lookout for a **jewel thief**. Two of them are chatting, and another one is giving someone directions. I guess the police

think they have the thief in custody already.

We search the crowds for the granny lady as we walk. Just as I start to worry that maybe this is a **waste** of time and isn't going to help, I see it. A **flash** of green and pink. Then it's gone.

"Milo, Mindy, Manny, did you all see that? It's her!" I shout above the music coming from the stage.

"No, where?" Mindy asks.

I point in the direction of the glimpse of green. There it is again. This time we all see it. The back of a head, in a green and pink chunni. It **must** be her!

"She's walking away – we have to follow!" I say.

"Ooh, a high-speed chase!" says Milo excitedly. Samosa woofs in agreement.

"Not exactly high-speed, Milo, with all these people in our way." Mindy sighs as we try to push our way through the crowd.

We can't let our suspect get away though. If this is the woman on the cap-cam recording, she might be the **real** thief who stole the diamond!

CHAPTER TEN

FOLLOW THAT GRANNY!

"There she is, I see her! Just act casual and don't get too close," I say, as we head after the granny in the green and pink chunni.

We follow her for about ten minutes, getting further away from the main festival crowds. Where is she going?

She takes a left down a side road and crosses over to a large stone-coloured building. Wait, the **mandir**?

"What's a **mandir**, Neesh?" asks Milo, reading the big lettering across the front of the building as we watch the granny walk in through the entrance.

"It's the temple. Well, we'll have to go in after her!" I say. "We can't go in there!" Manny protests. "Won't it look strange, a bunch of kids in the mandir without adults?"

"We **HAVE** to go in there," I say. "The police aren't looking for any other granny because they think they have the culprit. But what if this granny knows something? What if she's the **thief**!?"

Milo nods. "Neesh is right. We have to do this for Granny Jas."

I smile gratefully at Milo. "Look, there's a side door. We can sneak in there and hopefully catch whoever is inside by surprise. At the very least we might see or hear some **evidence**!"

"**Stealth mode**!" Milo grins.

I give the side door to the mandir a gentle push. It's open! I pop my head round first to make sure there's no one there. The door leads straight into an empty corridor, so we all pile in. Milo gives Samosa a treat to keep her quiet. We don't want her giving us away. (Milo always keeps treats on him just in case, even though he doesn't own a dog!)

"Woah!" Milo whispers, staring in awe at all the religious symbols and statues.

"Better take our shoes off, it is a mandir," I remind everyone, so we remove our shoes and leave them in the compartments in the wall that are there just for that purpose. Judging by the number of shoes already here the mandir is pretty empty. It's lovely and cool in here and so quiet. I feel calm straight away.

"This is so amazing!" marvels Milo. "Look, the elephant god, Ganesh! I read all about him in that book Granny gave me," he says, proudly pointing to a painting on the wall.

"Bet you know more than me," Manny whispers back. "Maybe I should borrow that book."

Just then we hear some noise coming from behind a door at the end of the corridor. It sounds like shouting. We hurry towards it and press our ears against the door to **listen**.

Now we can hear sounds of muffled grunting and heavy feet on the floor. Something very odd is going on in that room. What's happening in there? My heart thuds in my ears along with the pounding on the other side of the door. I'm suddenly a bit **scared** but I know we can't give up now. I'm just gathering the courage to open the door slightly and have a look when it opens inwards and we all **fall** into the room in a heap!

"Ah, it seems we have some visitors," says a voice. "Grannies, **assemble**!"

We look up from the floor to see about **twenty** grannies lined up in front of us, standing with their arms outstretched, fists aimed at us in a martial-arts pose!

We scramble up and I desperately try to back us out of this situation. "Sorry, we've obviously made a mistake. We…um, thought this was the cinema!" I say, helplessly looking back at the door.

"No, we didn't. We know one of you grannies stole the famous diamond!" Milo steps forward – and then quickly steps back again when one of the grannies edges closer.

"I know **karate**!" says Manny.

Mindy nudges her brother. "No, you do not. You just watched that film and now you think you can do **flying kicks**."

Manny goes pink and hisses, "Well, they don't know that, do they?"

One of the grannies steps forward, chuckling. "No need to show us, young man. We're not going to hurt you and we certainly did not steal that jewel."

Wait, I recognize that voice.

"**Kangana!** From the B & B! What are you doing here?" I say stepping forward to stand in front of her.

She's the granny we followed here with the green and pink chunni! And now she's facing us

I can see she's not the woman from the cap-cam footage at all. Kangana is the same height as my Granny.

I think back to the cap-cam footage and the height of that woman against the sign on the wall. It's not Kangana!

Kangana smiles and says, "Welcome to the **SHSG**!"

"The **SHSG**?" we all repeat at the same time.

"Like the name at the B & B?" I ask.

"Yes and no. This is the headquarters of the **SHSG**, which stands for **THE SECRET HINDU SOCIETY OF GRANNIES**. The B & B is how I make a living but I am the founder of the SHSG as well," Kangana explains. "We look after our communities, we protect the vulnerable and we keep a close eye on any dodgy business."

"Wow – but how?" I ask.

Kangana looks at the other grannies. "I think it's time we got you children back to your parents. Come along."

"No, we can't go back yet!" I say. "We have to save my Granny Jas. She's been **arrested** for stealing that diamond and she didn't do it. If you are a society of grannies, you should want to **help** her!"

Kangana sighs. "I was horrified to hear they arrested your granny. The police have really bumbled this one. Okay, you must listen carefully and everything you see and hear must stay a secret! Sit and I will tell you everything."

We all nod **solemnly** and sit down on the floor.

Kangana speaks quietly and slowly. "Think of the last time you went to the supermarket or the post office or the park. Nobody notices a kindly old granny sitting on a bench. You think she's just having a little rest, maybe, or enjoying the fresh air. **Wrong!** She is most likely conducting surveillance, watching out for any trouble. People think once we get past a certain age we are useless, only good for rolling the roti or folding washing. But we grannies decided that between us we have the best knowledge of what goes on in our own neighbourhoods and that intelligence should be put to good use. The **SHSG** is a secret network of crime stoppers!"

Milo whistles, impressed. "So, you're kind of like the Avengers, but the **granny** version?"

Kangana chuckles. "Yes, I suppose we are. Only **better**." She winks.

"I love it!" Manny claps his hands together. "This is so **awesome**!"

Mindy shakes her head in disbelief. "This is **wild**!"

I lean back on my hands, trying to make sense of everything that's happening. This really *is* wild. Secret granny societies, diamond thieves, my granny arrested. Everything feels like it's moving too fast – I can't keep up.

Kangana sees my face and touches my arm sympathetically. "We always patrol any major events in the city, and we were keeping an eye on the diamond the whole time. But whoever took it was too quick for us. I just don't understand how on earth they got past us." Kangana shakes her head. "We're as **puzzled** as you are."

Just then something Kangana said before clicks in my brain. That makes so much sense!

"Maybe it's like you said, Kangana – no one

notices a granny! I mean, there were **A LOT** of grannies at the festival. We already know someone who looked like Granny was outside the museum – we thought it was you, but we know now it wasn't. What if it was someone disguised as a granny? And if that's right, who was it and where did they go after they **stole** the diamond? Someone could have seen them but not realized they were in **disguise!**"

Kangana thinks. "That's an interesting theory. I do remember something now, Anisha. I was patrolling the festival this morning when I noticed a granny with a similar green and pink chunni to mine. And I remember thinking, **She has good taste in chunnis**. She was with two teenage girls and she was near the staging area. Anyway, later, when the alarm went off at the museum, I was making my way through the crowd and I saw that granny let herself into the festival office with one of those swiping **pass cards**. I didn't have time to think any more about it because then the police arrived, and I went straight up to the museum to see what had happened."

Milo, Mindy, Manny and I all look at each other and say, "**A clue!**"

"**Wait**," I add, a memory suddenly jolting back to me. "**A granny with two girls**... Were these girls quite similar-looking, Kangana? Did they have the same hair and clothes?"

Kangana nods curiously.

"It's that **family** again! Remember, I told you, Milo? **The Patels!** We met them in the service station and they were a bit shifty and nervous. Then I overheard the dad having that weird conversation about them coming to Leicester and not being recognized. Now do you believe me that they're **suspicious**?"

"I think it's definitely a reason to **investigate**," Milo answers solemnly.

"Okay, tell me **everything** you know," Kangana says. "The **SHSG** won't let you down!"

CHAPTER ELEVEN

SMELLY SAMOSAS

I explain the whole **story**, right from the beginning when we passed the Patels on the road, to the **weird** meeting at the service station and the **suspicious** phone call and then later seeing the dad at the festival and the cap-cam footage of the woman with the wire cutters. Kangana nods. Milo fidgets, because he's already heard this twice now, but Mindy and Manny listen without interrupting for once.

"So, you see, they're **prime suspects**," I conclude. "But why would they have a pass to access the festival office? Could they have stolen that too?"

"Maybe they hid the diamond in there?" Mindy

suggests. "They can't just wander around holding the world-famous diamond, can they? So they hide it in the one place no one will look. Who would think to search the organizers' office?"

She's right, it's **perfect**! Mindy is a pretty good detective.

"Okay, so we need to get back over to the festival, somehow get into that office and search it," I say.

Just then Manny's phone rings. It's his dad, Uncle Tony.

"I'd better answer it." He grimaces. "Hi, Dad… Yeah, we're still at the festival. Can we stay out a bit longer? …**Ohhh**, but we're not hungry… **But**… **Oh okay**, Dad. We'll head back now." Manny sighs and ends the call.

"We have to go back?" I ask.

"Yeah. Dad says they've ordered some food and we have to eat while it's warm. I think it's just an excuse to get us back, to be honest. I could hear Bindi in the background telling him what to say.

She's worried about us," Manny explains.

"But we have to investigate that clue! We haven't got any time to waste!" I don't mean to shout but we can't give up now.

Kangana pats my shoulder. "Calm down, **beta**. Listen, we'll carry on **investigating** here. It might be that one of our operatives remembers something else. And we'll use our connections in the city to find out who is on the organizing team for the festival and who might have access cards to that office. The more evidence we have, the better chance of getting Jaswant out of jail. Now, you go back to the B & B. Your parents might have news from the police station this evening and then tomorrow we can regroup. I'll be serving you breakfast, so we can catch up then."

I agree **reluctantly**. Milo, Mindy, Manny and I say our goodbyes to the grannies of the **SHSG** and leave the mandir. Samosa the dog has fallen asleep, so Milo wakes her gently and carries her

back to the B & B. Kangana says Samosa can stay
with us tonight.

"She's a bit **whiffy**,
Milo. You **ARE**
going to give
her a wash,
aren't you?"
asks
Mindy,
pinching
her nose.

"Shush,
you'll hurt her
feelings! But yes,
I might just give her quick rinse down in the bath,"
says Milo, scrunching his nose up too.

I trail behind a bit and Manny walks by my side.
"You okay, Anisha?" he asks.

"I just wish we could solve this now and get
Granny Jas home," I say, frustrated.

"I know, we all do, but we have to do this properly or we could make things **worse**," says Manny. "We're here for you, Anisha. And for Granny Jas."

I smile then. I'm missing Granny *so much*, but I'm not alone. We're going to do this together.

We get back to the B & B and manage to **sneak** Samosa into our room without anyone in the family seeing. We take off our coats, wash our hands and then head into Aunty Bindi and Uncle Tony's room. They've ordered some samosas (which makes Milo smile), mixed grill and naan, and even though I'm worried about Granny I realize I'm starving, so I eat a plateful. Milo sneaks some food in a napkin for the dog to have later.

Uncle Tony says we should keep busy and makes us all help him unload the minibus, which takes **longer** than you'd think. Aunty Bindi has packed enough stuff for a six-week holiday!

Finally at around **6 p.m.**, Mum and Dad return from the police station, alone.

"No Granny?" I ask.

Dad shakes his head sadly. "Not yet, **beta**, but she's okay and she said to tell you not to worry. We hope she'll be home tomorrow, but first they have to eliminate her from the investigation."

"What does that mean?" Milo asks.

"It means they haven't **ruled** her out," I say. "It means they still think she did it."

"But surely there will be CCTV footage from the museum that shows that Granny didn't take the jewel?" Mindy says.

Dad exchanges a look with Mum, which I know means they have bad news to tell us.

"Well, you see, it seems that there **is no CCTV** footage."

"**WHAT?!!!**" Milo, Mindy, Manny and I all yell.

"**SHHH,**" Mum says. "There are probably other people staying here too, you know!"

"I'm sorry, but **what**?" I whisper-shout. "How is that **possible**? That exhibition had the most **valuable** jewel we've ever had in the East Midlands and they **didn't** have cameras watching it?"

"They did, but they weren't **working** at the time of the theft," Dad explains.

"**Sabotage**!" gasps Milo. "I bet someone hacked into their system and uploaded a virus that corrupted their network."

"Well, no. Much simpler than that, actually," says Dad. "They've discovered that someone **snipped** the wires to the camera."

"Ah, old school," says Milo knowingly.

"**Wire cutters**, Milo," I say meaningfully.

"Wait, what? Oh, like the—" But Milo doesn't get to finish his sentence, because Manny nudges him.

Dad looks at us quizzically. "Like the what?"

I smile **sweetly**. "Oh, nothing, Dad, you know Milo." I roll my eyes for effect.

As usual, that's answer enough, and Dad moves on to telling us about the law and what the procedures are when someone gets arrested. As the others sit and listen, I open up Mindy's notepad. Circling where I wrote **Granny in green chunni**, I add "**??**"

CHAPTER TWELVE

ON A MISSION

It's seven o'clock the next morning when I'm woken by the smell of coffee **wafting** up from downstairs in the B & B. I feel like I've barely slept and my eyes fight to stay open. Then I remember and it all floods back to me – my granny, in **jail** for something she **didn't do**.

I get up quickly and pull some clothes on, not even bothering to take my pyjamas off first. Layers are good, **right**?

I nudge Mindy awake and then I run to the bathroom to brush my teeth and splash some water on my face. I go across the hall to Mum and Dad's room to see if they're up. I can hear them talking before I go in.

"I think you need to calm down, darling. Your aura is very **red** and not in a good way. We need to **meditate**. Look, we can sit here and just take a moment while it's quiet," Mum says.

"I need to get to the police station, is what I need to do. They could be interrogating Mum, and I should be with her," Dad says. "You know what she's like – she might say something innocently that gets her into even more trouble!"

"No, I don't think so. She's very smart, your mother," Mum says. "But there **IS** a great big **jewel** missing, and she is their only suspect at the moment. You know, not much can worry me but this...it really worries me."

Dad sighs loudly. "Me too. But we have to do something."

They both sound so anxious I decide to go in and tell Mum and Dad what we've learned so far. I push the door open. Mum and Dad stare at me in shock.

I stare back – with good reason.

They are both sitting on the floor at the end of their bed. Mum is sitting cross-legged with both hands together in a prayer pose. Dad is doing a headstand with his legs crossed!?!? I shake my own head to make sure I'm not seeing things. Nope, he's definitely on his head. I didn't even know he could do that!

Forgetting completely what I came in to say, I mutter, "**Um**, what are you doing?"

"Oh, hello, Anni dear, we're just about to start meditating. It's very good in times of stress, you know," Mum says.

Dad turns the right way up with a small groan and smiles weakly at me. "Alright, Anni? Don't look so shocked! I used to be *very* nimble, I'll have you know. I was **gymnastics champion** for my school. I really wanted to compete in the Olympics one day, but then I hurt my knee and that was that. I wonder if I can still backflip?" he says wistfully.

"Really? I thought you always wanted to study law," I say. It's weird to think my parents had other **dreams** once, like me.

"Oh, I had lots of big plans when I was your age, Anni. Anyway, no time for that now. Go on, go and get some breakfast so your mum and I can get ready. I need to get to the police station to check on Granny."

Dad shoos me back out of the room and I shut the door, thinking how **wonderfully odd** my parents are sometimes.

A little while later we head down to breakfast. Kangana gives us a **thumbs up** when our parents aren't looking. Milo, Mindy, Manny and I sit at a separate table from the grown-ups. We all wolf down some cereal and croissants as we come up with a plan for the day.

Kangana arrives at the grown-ups' table with another pot of chai and then looks sideways at us.

I clear my throat. "**Um**, Mum, would it be **alright** if Milo, the twins and I go back to the festival today?" I ask.

"Well, okay but I'd rather you went with a grown-up. I don't want you children wandering around for the whole day by yourselves, Anni. It's very busy and if there's a jewel thief on the loose, who knows what else is out there!" Mum frowns.

"We'll take them," Aunty Bindi offers.

"**Oh, no!**" I shout a little too quickly. "I mean, didn't you want to check out that dress shop, Aunty? Remember, you've got that big wedding to go to next year and you wanted a really nice **outfit** to wear. It might take your mind off things."

Uncle Tony smiles. "That's really thoughtful, Anisha, but who will keep you lot out of **trouble?**"

Kangana speaks up. "I could. I mean, I'm going to the festival anyway, I don't mind watching them for a couple of hours. They can come with me to the mandir as well. I volunteer there every day in the kitchens."

"Oh, I don't know, we couldn't impose like that," Mum says. "You've only just met us, after all."

"I understand your hesitation," Kangana replies, "but I'd like to help. You obviously have a lot to deal with at the moment. You can take down my number at the mandir in case you need to reach us," she assures them.

"Well, Manny and Mindy have mobile phones anyway. Ah, what do you think, Tony? It would be good for them, no?" Dad answers. "Kids today need to know what a little hard work looks like. Being selfless is a good life lesson!"

Tony thinks for a second. "Yes, it's fine with me. I'm always saying the children need to know what a day's work looks like!"

And so it's agreed. We pretend to moan but secretly we're all **grinning** inside. A few hours, parent-free, to investigate, solve this mystery and clear Granny's name. If we can do all that, and still go on our trip to the Space Centre tomorrow, we might be able to save this family holiday after all!

CHAPTER THIRTEEN

OPERATION PARALLELOGRAM

As soon as the grown-ups are out of the way, we head over to the mandir with Kangana. This time we go through the front entrance and we take Samosa with us. Thankfully Milo bathed her last night after all the grown-ups had gone to sleep. I think she quite liked it. She liked shaking all the water over us afterwards anyway!

Kangana leads us to a different room this time, a small one with a desk and chair and a huge bookshelf behind it.

"Welcome to my office," she says.

Milo, Mindy, Manny and I look at each other

and then around the room. On the wall to the left of us is a huge noticeboard. On it is a poster showing combat moves, an advert for a neighbourhood family fun day, a list of the top ten surveillance tactics, and a recipe for Granny M's special healing dal* to be consumed after any injury. I don't know who Granny M is, but I want to meet her.

"Shouldn't we be heading to the festival office?" I ask. "We need to see if the Patel granny hid the jewel there."

"All in good time, beta. First, we need a few things," she answers and hands Milo and Manny a package each. "We didn't find anything else out last night, so it is imperative we are prepared so we can make the most of any opportunity that arises to hunt for clues and evidence."

"Ooh, are these geothermal trackers? Or laptops?

---

* Dal is a dish made from lentils. There's yellow dal, red dal and even green dal. The green one is a bit yucky, but Granny Jas makes me eat it. It's good for me, apparently. Why is it that all the yucky-looking foods are "good for us"?

Perhaps special **phone-cloners**?" Manny asks enthusiastically.

"Pah, we don't need any of that," Kangana scoffs. "Listen, do you think we know how to use all that new-fangled **technobobbly**? No, we use our **instincts**, our **common sense.** I tell you, if some of these world leaders used a little less **bobbly** and a bit more **brains**, the world would be a far better place."

She sounds like my Granny Jas and it makes me smile.

Manny laughs as he opens his parcel. "I can't wear this!"

"You must and you will!" says Kangana. "If we are going to investigate at the festival, we may need a **distraction**."

Milo and Manny take the items from the packages and put them on over their other clothes. Then they turn to look at each other, giggling uncontrollably. They are each wearing a grey wig with a chunni over the top, and a salwar kameez. They look like little old grannies!

"You look so different, Milo," Manny says.

"You too. This is fun!" laughs Milo.

"This is not fun, this is serious. Remember why we are doing this," Kangana tells them, but it doesn't stop them giggling. I have to admit, they look pretty **hilarious**. Mindy takes photos on her phone while they pose and make silly faces.

Kangana tells them to settle down and then asks me, "So what's the plan?"

"Well, we need to get over to the festival. Maybe ask around, see if anyone else saw this **mystery** granny in the green and pink chunni. We also need to get into the festival office and search it, in case the **Patels** really did leave the diamond there to collect later. Why else would the Patel granny have been seen going in there? And we need to keep a lookout for any more clues," I say.

"Easy-peasy." Milo smiles.

"Okay, that's settled then. Next, we need a code name for this covert operation. Any ideas?" Kangana asks us.

Manny sticks his hand up straight away. "**Operation Code-Cracker!**" he declares.

"There's no code to crack, Manny." Mindy rolls her eyes at her brother's suggestion. "How about **Operation Rogue Grannies**?" she says with a flourish.

Milo offers one up next. "What about **Operation Find the Jewel and Prove Granny's Innocence?**"

"Too long, Milo," I say, but it gives me an idea. "How about **Operation Parallelogram**?"

"How did you go from what Milo said to a word I can't even pronounce?" laughs Mindy.

I explain: "We're looking for a stolen jewel. A diamond is a type of jewel, but it's also a mathematical shape. And the diamond shape is one type of **parallelogram**. Get it? A code name for an operation is supposed to be difficult to understand. No one else will know what we mean if we mention it outside of this room. It's **perfect**!"

Mindy, Milo, Manny and Kangana all look at each other and then back to me. They start to **chuckle** and I feel my cheeks getting hot.

"We don't have to use it," I say.

Kangana steps forward. "No, **beta**, we're not laughing at you. Your granny would be proud of you. You have a very logical mind, which has come up with the most perfect solution when we need it. **Operation Parallel-o-whatsit**, it is!"

CHAPTER FOURTEEN

THE TRUTH ABOUT THE PATELS!

When we get to the festival, it's still quiet as it's pretty early. Milo and Manny are in **disguise** because no one really **notices** grannies and we might need them to blend in. They hang back with Kangana and join the small crowd by the stage. I see Bhoomi Biddum, the organizer who we met yesterday, straight away. She's still wearing that enormous headset and carrying her clipboard. I wave and she gestures for Mindy and me to come over, so we do. It occurs to me that maybe she can help us with our enquiries.

"How are you, darlings? Any news on your

grandmother yet? Such a terrible business," she says as she air-kisses us.

"No, Bhoomi, but could we ask you a couple of questions? It might help Granny Jas," I reply.

"Of course, darling, ask away. Anything I can do..."

"Well, we were wondering who has access to the festival office. Is it just you or do other people have passes?" I ask.

Bhoomi frowns. "Just myself and my assistant Parvesh. Why do you ask? You don't think our team had anything to do with this?"

Mindy answers quickly. "No, not at all, we're just following up on a couple of things we saw on our friend's cap-cam."

"Cap-cam, what's **that**?" Bhoomi smiles in **confusion**.

"Oh, it's a cap with a camera on it. Our friend Milo caught quite a bit of the **action** on it yesterday, though not the theft itself, unfortunately," I say.

"You'll have to show me this cap-cam sometime – technology is so **advanced** these days. Anyway, I must dash, girls, the festival won't run itself!" Bhoomi says, and with that she hurries off.

"Oh, we didn't even get to ask her if she saw the granny with the green chunni!" Mindy moans. "What now?"

Just then music starts up on the stage – an old Bollywood song. Some dancers come out and prance around like they do in the films Aunty Bindi loves. The crowd in front of the stage cheer and clap. That's when I see it. The green chunni with the pink pattern on the edges! I grab Mindy's sleeve.

"Look, it's her – the **Patel** granny! Well, the back of her head – but it's got to be her!"

"**No way!** She's brave, coming back to the festival and just walking around like that where anyone could see her," Mindy remarks.

"Remember, she doesn't know we know she's

the thief. Well, we don't know if she **IS** the thief, but we **definitely** know she was on that footage. **And** Kangana saw her around the time of the theft heading into the festival office – a **locked** office that no one except Bhoomi and her assistant should have access to. So either way, she has some **explaining** to do."

"What do we do? Should we **confront** her?" Mindy asks. "Should we signal Kangana, Milo and Manny to come over?"

"No, let's get closer and see who she's with first," I say.

So we sneak a bit nearer…and see from behind that she's talking with Parvesh, the festival assistant with the purple jacket who told off the bhangra dancers! **What?** Is he in on it too? Maybe he gave her the pass key to the office. That makes **sense**! There's no time to waste. I don't bother to listen to what they're talking about – it's time to **confront** this granny and get to the truth.

I step forward and say, "Stop, thief! I'm making a **citizen's arrest**!", just like they do on one of Aunty Bindi's Bollywood soaps.

Mindy looks at me, like, **What on earth are you doing?** but she steps forward too and says, "Um, yes, we are, what she said – stop and surrender!"

Parvesh turns around abruptly. "**What the...?**" he starts. And at that point, the granny turns around too.

Except, she looks **different** now. What is going on?! Is this the right woman? She's got the green chunni with the pink pattern on her head but she's not wearing a salwar kameez or a sari. She's wearing **jeans** and a **T-shirt** with the words **Bollydreamers** and a photo of a band emblazoned across it. Her hair isn't grey any more either. In fact, she doesn't look like an old lady like at the service station or on the cap-cam footage. Now – she just looks my mum's age. Could she have been wearing make-up and a wig to make her look **old** before, or something?

Parvesh folds his arms and glares at us. "What is your problem?"

Suddenly my throat closes up and I can't speak. I have an awful **sinking** feeling that we've got this very very wrong.

Just then, the brightly coloured light cannons on the stage flicker and the music builds. There's quite a crowd gathered – at least a couple of hundred people, with more arriving, and they shout and cheer.

A voice booms out over the tannoy: "Ladies and gentlemen, it's almost time for our very special guests. For the first time in the UK, here on a surprise and top-secret visit, please put your hands together and make some noise...let's give a very warm Leicester welcome to the **BOLLYDREAMERS**!"

Parvesh leans towards us and mutters through gritted teeth, "I'll deal with you two in a moment." Then he smiles at the woman, who is clearly **not** a granny, and they watch the stage.

Just then the **BOLLYDREAMERS** come out onstage. First a young man, probably in his early twenties, wearing tight trousers and a red shirt. His sleeves are rolled up and on his lower left inside arm is a tattooed line of **stars**. I've seen something like that before, I think! He starts singing and then two girls around the same age come out dancing and singing too. They look really familiar. It takes me a minute and then...**OH!** "It's **them**!" I shout, pulling on Mindy's arm.

"Who? The **BOLLYDREAMERS**? I know, they're Bindi's favourite band. She'll be gutted she missed them," Mindy replies.

"No, it's **THEM,**" I say. "They're the **PATELS**!"

It's all coming back to me now. Aunty Bindi waving her magazine at me and saying we should go and see this band and something about there being a rumour they were coming to the UK. The glimpse of the tattooed stars on the dad's arm and now he's on stage! The Bollydreamers and the Patels are the same people!

"I think I may have got it wrong about the diamond," I admit. "I think they might have been in disguise for another reason."

The woman standing with Parvesh – who it seems is NOT a granny at all – turns to me. "Good, aren't

they? I'm Rhadika, by the way, their tour manager."
She holds out her hand. "Now what's all this about
a **citizen's arrest**?"

Parvesh jumps in. "They were joking, part of a
performance or something. **WEREN'T YOU!**" he says,
eyebrows raised.

"I'm **really** sorry!" I stutter. "I didn't know who
you were. I mean, we saw you in disguise at the
service station, but obviously we didn't **know** they
were disguises then. You were all so **secretive** and
suspicious when we met you, and then I overheard
Mr Patel – I mean, your lead singer – on the phone
and he said he didn't want the police involved and
I noticed he was wearing a wig. Anyway, when the
jewel was **stolen**, and we saw someone we thought
was **you** by the museum right at the time of the
robbery, well, I put two and two together and got—"

"It wrong!" Parvesh shouts. "I've never heard
anything so **ridiculous**. I must apologize, Rhadika!"

"No **harm** done, it's quite **funny** really,"

Rhadika says. "We wore the disguises to avoid attracting attention but somehow we ended up doing the opposite and making ourselves suspects in a jewel heist! And actually, I haven't even had a chance to go round the rest of the festival yet. I was looking forward to seeing the diamond too! Wait till I tell the group about all this confusion we've caused!" she chuckles.

I go a bit pink and look sideways at Mindy. "Well, this is embarrassing. But in our defence there seem to be a lot of women wearing that same green chunni with the pink patterned edge!" I smile sheepishly.

I can feel Parvesh glaring at us, but Rhadika just smiles. "It takes a brave person to admit they got it wrong and I can see how our behaviour might have seemed strange. The **BOLLYDREAMERS** have been on tour in America and we had a few spare days, so when the festival invited us, we thought why not! But there's always such a **fuss** with the press and the group **hate** all that, so we decided to travel in quietly and in disguise. The police just complicate matters when you're trying to stay under the radar." She winks at me.

"So the disguises were so you wouldn't be recognized?" Mindy asks.

"Exactly," Rhadika replies.

"My stepmum loves the **BOLLYDREAMERS**," Mindy adds. "I know it's a bit cheeky after we just tried to arrest you, but do you think we could get their autographs for her?"

Rhadika laughs. "You're a **gutsy** pair, I like you. The band are performing again later. Come back around 7 p.m. and we'll sort it out for you."

If we ever manage to solve this mystery, I think to myself. I feel a bit silly and disappointed – I thought we were so close! **What now?**

CHAPTER FIFTEEN

THE TOP SECRET PHONE CALL

Mindy chatters away excitedly to Rhadika as the band continues to play and the crowd around us goes wild. I just really want to get out of here. I need to think about what we do next. Granny is **still** locked up and we're no closer to finding the **jewel** or the **thief**.

"Mindy, we'd better go. We still need to…you know." I jerk my head towards the edge of the crowd.

"Ah yes, it was nice to meet you anyway," Mindy says to Rhadika as I try to drag her away. "She's **SO** nice!" Mindy whispers to me.

We're just leaving when one of the festival stewards approaches Parvesh, who was still watching the **BOLLYDREAMERS**, and says, "Hey, look – I've got these wire cutters. Someone handed them in at the information desk. Where are we leaving lost property?"

Parvesh stares at the wire cutters **in horror** then glances at us and snatches them from the steward.

"I'll take them!"

And he stomps off to the festival office.

"That was rude!" comments Mindy.

"It was, but did you see what she gave him? **Wire cutters!** We know the wires to the CCTV cameras at the museum were cut." My tummy does an **excited** flip like it always does when something is about to happen.

"They could have belonged to anyone!" reasons Mindy.

"Maybe, but why would he react like that?" I reply. "You said it yourself, the thief might have **hidden** the jewel in the one place no one would think to look. We need to get inside that office. I thought all was lost, but that clue just landed in our laps. We can't ignore it!"

"But Parvesh just went in there. How do we get him out?" asks Mindy – and then she smiles. "**Wait!** I think I know. We have the **perfect** granny distraction!"

She points at Milo and Manny across the road, before filling me in on the plan. Then Mindy runs over to brief Milo, Manny and Kangana, while I hide behind a large plant pot outside the festival office door.

A few minutes later, and our plan is put into motion.

"What did you say?" Manny shouts loudly, in a grannyish voice.

"Um, you heard me. And I'd say it again!" Milo replies.

"If I'd heard you, I wouldn't have asked what you'd said, would I?" Manny exclaims.

"Well, you should have been listening, and then you wouldn't have to ask what I said, would you?" Milo yells as they start the performance of their lives.

Manny shoves a nearby pop-up banner and it falls over. I sense the crowd around them going quiet watching the best pretend argument I've ever seen.

"I'm so sick of you...you...you bad granny friend!" Manny screams in a high-pitched voice as he hitches up his salwar kameez and stands in a battle pose.

"Yeah? Well, I've had enough of you too!"

Milo screeches back, flinging his chunni over his shoulder and cracking his knuckles threateningly. He sounds really convincing! I must tell both of them to sign up for drama club at school – they're really good actors. Samosa barks and jumps up around them adding to the **chaos**. Soon everyone is watching as their fake granny fight unfolds.

Just a few seconds later Parvesh **storms** out of his office. "What on earth is going on out here!" he yells, and I take my opportunity to sneak in. I **creep** up the small steps and look around to make sure no one's **watching**. I spot Mindy, who is keeping a lookout. She gives me a thumbs up. I put my hand nervously on the handle and push it down, nudging the door open. Quickly I **slip in** and shut the door behind me.

Inside, there are two desks – one with a toolbox on top of it, the **wire cutters**

168

placed next to it. There's a **cheesy** photo of Parvesh and an older lady in a frame sitting there too, so I guess that must be Parvesh's desk. Hurriedly, I check his desk drawers. Just paper clips and Post-it notes in the top one. The second one has deodorant, a razor, a hand mirror and strawberry lip balm. The bottom one is more interesting – a copy of a book titled **Ten Steps to Taking Your Boss's Job**.
YIKES!

Just then I hear Mindy's warning call. We'd agreed she would **woof** like a dog if Parvesh was coming back this way. Her woofing sounds more like a bear with a sore head, but I get the point she's making. I hear footsteps and Parvesh shouting, "Now keep it down, will you!"

I quickly duck under the other desk, which must belong to Bhoomi. It's only a small space, so I have to curl right up with one knee pushed against my ear and the other leg stuck awkwardly underneath me.

The door to the office opens and I can see the trouser legs and feet of Parvesh enter and then disappear behind his desk as he sits down. I hear him fiddling about with papers and then he opens his desk drawer and, after a moment, says to himself, "You really are the **best**, Parvesh, never mind what that silly Bhoomi says." He must have the mirror out.

Then he starts singing that old song, **"You're Simply The Best!"**

I cover my mouth to stifle a **giggle**. What a funny man!

Thankfully, his phone rings before I give myself away. "Hello?" he answers. "Oh, it's you…"

I strain to hear the voice on the other end of the phone but they're too quiet. I wonder who he's talking to.

He carries on. **"Yes, I've got it… Yes, yes, don't worry. I'll be there, 4.30 p.m. at the jeweller's. It's called Shah Jahan, isn't it?… No, I haven't told anyone. Top secret!"**

He laughs then, says goodbye and hangs up.

I can't believe what I've heard. **Top secret!** It must be him! He did get very shifty about the wire cutters and he **is** organizing some kind of meeting at a jeweller's later. He **stole** the diamond and now he's planning to **sell** it! He could have used his wire cutters to cut the cables to the CCTV, disguised as a granny wearing a **green chunni**, then come back to the office and hidden the jewel here until he could move it later. Parvesh must have dropped the cutters in the chaos that followed.

I have to tell the others, and right away, but how do I get out of here? I realize my hands are shaking. I'm stuck in here with an **actual** criminal. I need to stay calm.

What would Granny Jas do?

Luckily before I can come up with anything, there's a knock at the door. It's the steward from earlier.

"Yes, what is it?" Parvesh calls out.

"Um, it's just me again. They need you backstage. One of the dancers is having a **meltdown**."

"Can't Bhoomi deal with it?" Parvesh asks.

"We've tried to contact her, but I think there's something wrong with her headset. Nothing happens – the line just crackles," answers the steward.

I keep my fingers **crossed** that Parvesh will just

get up and go because my leg is starting to **cramp** from being all bent up under this desk.

Parvesh sighs. "Okay, I'm coming," he moans. "I'm always covering for her, though. She's never where she's supposed to be. And anyway, I have an **important** errand to run today, so at **4 p.m.** I'm out of here, no matter what happens." And he stomps off out the door.

Once Parvesh leaves I have a quick last look round the office, checking Bhoomi's desk too. Apart from that, there are no cupboards or cabinets to hide the jewel in, so I think Parvesh must have it on him now.

I go to the door and push the handle down cautiously, looking around outside quickly before running to Milo, Mindy, Manny and Kangana, who are waiting for me across the street. It's busier now so they blend in easily, and Milo and Manny's earlier disruption has been forgotten as the crowds mill about between the festival stands and around the stage. I weave through the people as quickly as I can, **dodging** elbows and small children.

When I get to them, Milo and Manny are mucking about, hitting each other with their chunnis, and Mindy and Kangana are deep in conversation about something.

"You'll never believe what I just heard!" I say, interrupting them all. "We have a new suspect to **investigate**!"

CHAPTER SIXTEEN

DODGY DIAMOND DEALS

After explaining everything I heard in the festival office to the others, we make a plan.

"Are we going to this Shah Jahan place to stop the dodgy diamond deal?" asks Milo excitedly.

"Should we call the police and tell them what we know?" asks Mindy cautiously.

"What if we're wrong though? We could get into trouble, right?" says Manny.

"We have to do something!" adds Kangana.

"We will do something," I say. "We'll go to the place Parvesh mentioned, and we'll watch from nearby. If it looks like it really is a dodgy deal, we'll

call the police and then be ready to pounce."

"Can we keep our granny disguises on?" asks Milo. "I quite like mine!"

"Yes, if you want to," says Kangana. "And I shall call a few of my very best **SHSG** to be on standby in case things get out of hand and Parvesh tries to make a run for it. We might need their kung-fu skills."

"Oh yes, good idea!" I agree.

And that's how a little while later, after some more mission-planning, we find ourselves **lurking** behind a bus stop opposite Shah Jahan, which turns out to be a quite posh-looking jewellery shop. It has

huge windows with big ledges outside full of
flowering plants.

"Isn't this a bit of a funny place to do a dodgy
deal? Not very private, is it?" Milo points out as
plenty of shoppers and festival goers walk by.
Samosa woofs in agreement.

"Unless you think no one would suspect a person
in a jewellery shop of making a dodgy deal," Mindy
points out. "It could be the perfect cover. I've seen
these documentaries with respectable-looking shop
owners doing under-the-counter deals. He could be
a fence."

"What's a **fence**?" Manny asks, confused.

"It's someone who deals in stolen goods,"
I answer as we watch the shop owner through
the window.

He certainly **looks** very respectable. He's an
older man, wearing glasses and a smart shirt. He
moves slowly around his shop, adjusting the displays
and helping customers. If it is a cover for his dodgy
dealings, it's a very convincing one.

Manny points at the Indian restaurant next door
to the jewellery shop. "The smell of all that lovely
food is making me hungry. Can we eat once we've
caught the thief and called the police? We missed
lunch and I'm **starving**!" he complains.

"Here, I have some **puri** in my bag, munch on
one of these," says Kangana as she pulls a steel tin
out of her tote bag. She opens it to reveal a pile of
small, perfectly round **puris**, a fried bread which my
Granny Jas often makes. The smell of them makes
me miss her. I've been concentrating hard on solving

this mystery and trying
not to think too much
about how much
Granny means to me.
But Kangana's **puris**
remind me so much of the
sort of thing Granny would
do in this situation. She
would be here, well prepared with snacks and
support. I blink and rub my eye.

"You okay, Neesh?" Milo asks as he chomps on
a **puri**.

"I'm okay, just thinking about Granny," I say.

"We've got this, Anisha," says Mindy. "Look how
close we are now!"

"And I don't mind stake-outs if we can have
snacks like this," says Manny.

Just then, I see Parvesh walking down the street.
"Look, he's here. Kangana, are your grannies in
position?"

179

"Yes, look." She points to the corner of the road opposite where two grannies are standing, pretending to have a chat as Parvesh passes them.

"And over there." She gestures to the other side of the street where a granny is sitting on a bench, seemingly having fallen asleep reading her book. She opens one eye and winks at us. The **SHSG** really are everywhere!

"I'm going to go into the shop. That Parvesh won't know who I am and I'll be able to see exactly what's going on," Kangana tells us.

We continue to watch as Parvesh goes into the jewellery shop. It's just him, the shop owner and two grannies. Wait! They're **SHSG** as well! I recognize one of them from the mandir. The shop is quite large and has a long counter which runs around the edge of the room. The shop owner beckons Parvesh over to one side, away from the others.

Kangana crosses over and enters the jewellery shop too while we watch. Then, as planned, the four of us plus Samosa scoot across the road, keeping our heads low – even though we get a strange look from a driver who stops to let us cross at the pelican crossing. **Safety first!**

We take up our positions, crouching under the ledge of the shop window, and pop our heads up through the leafy plants so we can see inside the shop. We can't see Parvesh's face because his back is turned to us, but the shop owner is smiling and holding something out to him that we can't see.

This **must** be it. I grab Mindy's arm. They're doing the deal now!

I see Kangana and one of her grannies in the background watching and it's clear she sees the handover happening too. They move closer.

"What are they **doing**, Anisha? I thought we were going to hang back!" Manny whispers.

My tummy **turns** – something's not right. I don't know how I know this, I just do. Why would Parvesh do this deal out in the open like this? Wouldn't they go into a back room or something?

"I've got a **terrible** feeling we've got this wrong..." I say, but it's too late. Kangana and the other two grannies launch themselves across the shop, pulling their best kung-fu attack poses, right as Parvesh turns with a box in his hand and opens it to reveal...a diamond.

But not the huge, famous, **stolen** diamond. This one is set in an **engagement** ring. He's buying an engagement ring.

I sink back down behind the plants.

"Oh, no!"

CHAPTER SEVENTEEN

SECRET SPARKLY CLUES

We race inside, where Kangana is now patting Parvesh on the head, straightening his collar and apologizing.

"So sorry, **beta**, just a mix-up! You carry on, this all looks very nice!" she chuckles nervously.

Parvesh looks like he remembers

184

me from earlier and then he looks confused and then annoyed. The shop owner looks even more irritated.

"I thought we were going to wait and see what happened," I mutter to Kangana.

"I know, **beta**, we just got a little carried away and it did look like there was something going on here."

"Sorry, could **someone** explain what's happening?" Parvesh asks.

"Yes, that would be nice," says the shop owner, snatching back the box with the ring in it.

I step forward. "I'll explain. I'm so sorry. We thought... Well, we got it wrong obviously, but...we thought **you** stole the diamond."

Parvesh splutters. "I did not! I'm going to pay for it!" he says, outraged.

"Not that diamond, silly," Kangana says. "The big diamond, the famous one!"

Now Parvesh looks horrified. "What? How **dare** you!"

"I'm **so** sorry, we really got it wrong. It's just that I overheard you on the phone making plans to meet someone about a diamond and I thought you were making a dodgy deal with the stolen jewel. And we **need** to find the culprit, because my granny is in **jail** and she didn't do it, but the police think she did!"

Parvesh looks at me and his face softens. "I can see you're really worried about your granny. To be honest, I would probably be the same if it was my **bibi**. She means everything to me. I keep her photo on my desk at work, she's my biggest supporter and she would want me to help you if I can." He scratches his head. "Okay, tell me. What made you think it was me?"

"Well, we have this cap-cam. It's my friend Milo's. This is Milo." I point at my best friend, who's still dressed as a granny.

Milo nods and smiles nervously at Parvesh.

I carry on talking too fast, but I have to get it all

out. "Anyway, on the footage it captured, we saw a woman dressed in a green chunni in the museum entrance right before the theft and she was carrying wire cutters. Then later we heard that **wire cutters** were used to cut the CCTV wires in the diamond exhibit. And then we saw a pair of wire cutters being handed back to you at the festival and you reacted so strongly, which made us think **you** might be the **diamond thief**."

Parvesh nods. "Ah, yes I had misplaced my wire cutters earlier in the day. I'd been using them on some floral displays. We event organizers use all kinds of tools to make everything look **fabulous**! I didn't want anyone to know I'd lost them, they'd take it out of my pay! So this cap-cam of yours – can I see the recording? I might notice something you haven't," he offers.

I look at Milo and Mindy, Manny and Kangana.

"It's worth a try," Milo says.

Milo and Manny set up the cap-cam and the

phone so Parvesh can see the footage. We all crowd round to watch it again too – even the jewellery-shop owner seems interested now he's stopped **huffing** at us. We get to the bit where we see the granny in the green chunni lurking by the museum entrance with the wire cutters in her hand. A look of **recognition** flashes across Parvesh's face.

"What is it?" I say.

"Pause the recording." Parvesh points. "That woman there..."

I look closely. We were so busy looking at the wire cutters in her hand last time that we didn't notice her shoes poking out from the bottom of her sari. But these are no **ordinary** shoes. These are red velvet boots with glinting silver heels and pointed, jewel-encrusted toes. I've only seen one pair of shoes like that ever.

I look from the screen to Parvesh. He **knows** it and I **know** it.

"What's wrong, Neesh? Your face has gone all strange," Milo says.

"It's Bhoomi Biddum," I say quietly. "It is, isn't it?" I look at Parvesh.

He shakes his head. "I think it is, but I don't

understand why she would do this. Bhoomi can be a lot of things but...a **thief**?"

"What? **No!** It can't be. How do you know?" Mindy asks.

"The shoes," I say. "Bhoomi wears those expensive-looking red boots with the spiky silver heels. Remember? How many grannies do you know who wear shoes like that? There can't be many! It has to be Bhoomi in disguise."

"I can't **believe** it." Parvesh has gone very pale.

"If it is her, we have to do something **now**," I say. "My granny spent a night in the police station yesterday because of all this. We have to expose the **truth**."

Kangana nods. "Stealing the diamond was bad enough, but disguising herself as one of us and letting your granny take the blame is even worse. She must be held accountable."

"How do we prove it though? We can't just accuse her," Parvesh says. "The footage doesn't show her stealing the diamond, it just shows she was there. So were a lot of other people. Plus she uses wire cutters as part of her job like I do making displays, so she can explain that away too."

We all slump a little. He's right. We don't have hard evidence. **Yet.**

Milo smiles at me. "That's all true. But no one messes with Granny Jas – so we're gonna need a plan, right, Neesh?"

I smile back at Milo. He's right. And we've been in trouble before and we always figure it out together. "Right," I say.

I think for a moment about everything we know about Bhoomi – which isn't that much.

"Let's watch a bit more of the footage," I suggest. "We missed the shoes the first time, so there might be something else we've missed."

We see Milo's view from the shoulders of the bhangra dancers and then Parvesh coming over to tell us off.

"Sorry about that!" Parvesh whispers. "Working with Bhoomi on this festival has been so **stressful**, I've been on edge all week!"

Then we watch the confusion and chaos as we realize something is happening over by the museum and push our way through the crowd. The cap is knocked off Milo's head and falls to the floor. We all lean in.

The camera is at a funny angle, pointing up from the floor. We see Granny being arrested and I can feel a lump in my throat. Then we see Bhoomi running over to us, all dishevelled.

I point to the screen. "There she is! It makes sense now why she looked like that, headphones all askew. She said she hadn't had a chance to visit the exhibition yet either, remember! She was lying. Why lie if you've got nothing to hide? She must have stolen the diamond, run off to hide it somewhere and then run back through the crowd as though she'd just found out. But where could she have hidden it?"

Parvesh nods. "Yes, you're right! She **DID** look dishevelled after the diamond was stolen. I don't know where she could have hidden it, but she wouldn't have had much time, so it **must** be nearby."

We turn back to the screen. This must be when Samosa picked up the cap and carried it over to us, as everything is filmed at her level and it's just legs and feet.

"You're such a good dog!" Milo smiles and pats her.

"She really is, Milo. Without Samosa we could have lost the cap-cam and all the footage on it!" Manny says.

And that's when I notice it. I pause the screen and rewind a bit. It's Samosa sniffing around on the ground a little way away from the cap-cam. She hasn't noticed it yet but it's still filming after falling off Milo's head. Samosa is snuffling her way through some leaves just by the entrance and then she nudges her nose against something **sparkly**. She uses her nose to uncover it. She nudges it again and picks it up with her teeth. Then she walks over to a nearby pot plant just inside the museum entrance and drops the earring into the soil, patting it with her paw. I pause the screen and rewind to where we can see the sparkly thing.

At first, I think it's just the light shining on a bit of foil or something.

"What is that?" I ask.

Milo touches the phone screen to zoom in and get a closer look at the shiny thing. We all tilt our

heads to try to see what it is. 
And then I realize.

"It's an earring! Right
there, on the floor outside
the museum – straight
after the diamond was
stolen," I say.

"Someone probably dropped
it." Milo shrugs.

"Yeah, but it's very distinctive," says Manny.

"We've seen that earring before," I say. "I'd
totally forgotten it till now. When we saw her after
Granny was arrested, Bhoomi was missing an
earring!"

Mindy looks at me. "Oh yeah!"

Parvesh looks closer and then grins. "That
confirms it then. She was definitely in the right place
at the right time!"

I smile too. "Bhoomi Biddum, we've got you
now!"

CHAPTER EIGHTEEN

THE TRAP

"I don't get it," Milo says. "So we have Bhoomi at the scene of the crime just before it happened with the wire cutters in her hand. Then later we see her earring on the ground near the entrance to the museum. But how do we **tie** it all together? It still feels like we don't have enough **proof**, Neesh."

I think for a moment and then I have it. "You're right, Milo, it's not enough on its own. But if we can come up with a plan to catch her at the scene of the crime, **THAT** might be enough! We'll need your help though, Parvesh, if this is going to work."

"I'll help any way I can." He nods.

"Us too!" agrees Kangana and her two undercover grannies.

"**Operation Parallelogram** is back on track!" Milo grins.

"**Operation Para-what?**" Parvesh asks.

"Never mind," I say. "Here's what we need you to do…"

A little while later, after making a phone call to Uncle Tony, we leave the jewellery shop and head back out into the festival. Parvesh runs off ahead as planned. It's still light outside and busier than before.

Milo and Manny have made up a game called **GRANNY WARS** and they play it all the way down the Golden Mile. It's basically just the two of them seeing who can run to the end of the road fastest (Manny), who can jump the furthest (Manny) and who can do a headstand for the longest (Milo), all while dressed as grannies. Samosa joins in by

running back and forth between them and **woofing** loudly.

Mindy rolls her eyes, but I can see she kind of wants to join in. I walk behind everyone else, my head **whirring** and my tummy turning.

We're supposed to be going to the Space Centre tomorrow. I really don't want to miss that trip but I *have* to clear Granny's name. I hope this plan works. It has to – it just *has* to.

When we get to the main festival area, Bhoomi is on the stage, bossing the crew around. We walk to the opposite end of the town square and pretend we're checking out a window display when we're **really** watching the reflection of what's happening behind us.

Uncle Tony and Aunty Bindi meet us there. "I knew you couldn't leave it alone!" she **scolds**, grabbing me and hugging me tight at the same time.

"I had to do something," I say. "It's Granny Jas – I couldn't just stand by while the police think she's a criminal! Let's move – quick behind here." I drag my family behind some **portaloos** for the festival goers. It's quieter here and we won't be seen. Mindy scrunches up her nose. "Bit **pongy!**"

Uncle Tony notices Milo and Manny's outfits. "Now what have we got here?" He chuckles.

"We're grannies in disguise!" Milo says proudly.

"Actually, we're kids disguised as grannies. We played a very **important** part in the solving of the case," Manny corrects him.

"Is that so?" Uncle Tony says. "Well, I'm proud of you all. Now what's this **top-secret** plan you've got?"

I look at Aunty Bindi. "We need your acting skills, Aunty. We need you to pretend to be a **blackmailer**."

"**WHAT?**" Uncle Tony says. "Who are we **blackmailing**?"

"Bhoomi Biddum, the woman we think **really** stole the diamond," I say.

"And what **exactly** am I asking her for?" Aunty Bindi says. I can tell she's **intrigued**.

"So, you're going to call her and say you know she **stole** the diamond, you have her **earring** from the scene of the crime, and if she doesn't pay you a **thousand pounds** you'll take the earring to the police."

"Will she go for that, do you think?" Uncle Tony asks.

"I do. If she's **guilty**, she won't want anything that could link her to the crime," I say.

"It's for Granny, so I'll do it," Aunty Bindi says. "But what happens then? We don't really have the earring, do we?"

"We arrange to meet her at the museum for the exchange of money for the earring and we get her to confess on camera. Parvesh, the assistant festival organizer, is speaking to the police right now. He has a friend on the force, Officer Winston," I explain.

"It's a **sting** operation!" Milo declares. "I've seen them on the telly on that police show I like."

"Right, okay, what number am I dialling?" Bindi asks as she pulls her huge bejewelled phone out of her bag and taps the screen.

I hand her the piece of paper Parvesh gave us with Bhoomi's mobile number on.

"Okay, give me a sec to get into character," Bindi says, turning away from us. "I'm a **mean criminal**," she mutters, jiggling her shoulders and shaking out her arms and legs like she's warming up for a run. She clears her throat, dials the number and switches to speakerphone.

We all look over to the stage where Bhoomi is as her mobile starts to ring. She stares at it for a second. Aunty Bindi has withheld her number so it will be coming up as unknown on Bhoomi's screen.

It suddenly occurs to me – what if she doesn't answer? The phone **rings** and **rings**, but then, just as I think it will go to voicemail, Bhoomi presses the button and lifts the phone to her ear. I turn to Aunty Bindi and nod.

She speaks in a weirdly **gruff** voice which takes us all by surprise. "Hello, is this Bhoomi Biddum? I have something of yours. Something you won't want the police to see. An earring."

I look back over to Bhoomi. She's frowning. "*Is this some sort of joke?*" we hear through the phone. "*Because I am not to be trifled with,*" she warns.

"Well," Aunty Bindi continues, "neither am I. Because I **WILL** take your earring to the police, and I'll tell them how I found it inside the museum exhibition just after that **lovely** big diamond was **stolen**. Don't think I won't. Unless, of course, you're willing to pay me to keep quiet."

Over on the stage, Bhoomi's face goes quite red with rage – I can even see it from here. *You have no proof that earring belongs to me,* she retorts.

"I don't think many people wear earrings like this one. You have a very distinctive style," Bindi replies in her gruff criminal voice. I'm not sure what TV shows she's been watching, but I can tell she's enjoying herself now. She **winks** at me while we wait for Bhoomi to answer.

After a pause, Bhoomi replies. *"Fine. I can meet you in one hour."*

Aunty Bindi grins at us, then says gruffly, "Inside the exhibition then. Make sure you're not followed."

Bhoomi says nothing and hangs up. We watch as she storms off the stage in the direction of the office.

"She believed it!" I whoop.

Uncle Tony hugs Aunty Bindi. "You were very convincing, my love. Should I be scared?"

"I was quite good, wasn't I?" Aunty Bindi **squeals**.

"So what now, Neesh?" Mindy asks me.

"Now, we **catch** a thief," I say.

CHAPTER NINETEEN

BACK TO THE SCENE OF THE CRIME

A short while later we're at the deserted museum, hiding and waiting. It's been closed off as a **crime scene** so there's no one else around except for us. Parvesh and his friend Officer Winston are waiting in the security room for Bhoomi's **confession**, along with the rest of my family. Milo, Mindy, Manny and I are all positioned behind the dinosaur display, just outside the room where the diamond exhibit was held. It's the best place to see what's going on in there without being seen, but it's not a very big display, so we're a bit squished together. It's quiet and dark. Milo switches his cap-cam on.

"This had better work!" Mindy mutters.

"My bum is going numb," moans Manny.

"My knees hurt," Milo adds.

"**Shhh!**" I say. "She could walk in at any second."

"Remind me how this is going to work again?" Manny asks, trying to shift position.

"Milo's cap-cam will film everything and it's streaming to the security room where Parvesh and the other police officers are all watching," I whisper. "Aunty Bindi will get Bhoomi to confess or at least say something to incriminate herself. That should be enough to get Granny Jas released!"

Just then, the door to the museum creaks open.

Someone's here!

We wait. The sound of clicking heels getting closer on the museum's wooden floors sends a **chill** up my spine.

She's covered her head in the green chunni, but I can still see her headset and the microphone poking out from underneath, so I know it's Bhoomi. She creeps into the room where the diamond case sits empty.

Aunty Bindi steps out of the shadows. She's dressed in a security uniform that Parvesh managed to get for us – a dark-coloured jacket and trousers, and a peaked cap, casting a shadow over her face. She keeps her distance from Bhoomi.

"Over here," she says in her deep, gruff voice.

Bhoomi swivels round. "Ah, there you are. I have your money, but I want to see the earring first."

Bindi doesn't move an inch. "Money first. After all, you are the one with something to hide. If the police knew you stole the diamond…"

Bhoomi doesn't take the **bait**. "I don't know what you're talking about. I just want my earring back. Now enough of this stalling, do you have it or not?"

I'm **nervous** for Aunty Bindi. Bhoomi is so **cunning** – who was I kidding? We can't get her to confess just like that.

But maybe, just maybe, flattery might work. I remember how much she liked it when we complimented the festival the first time we met her. She was keen to tell us **SHE** was the main organizer. If Bindi tells her how **great** her plan was, she might be tempted to **brag** again.

Bhoomi has her back to us and Aunty Bindi is facing in our direction. I try to signal and get her attention. Bhoomi is muttering something about this being a total waste of time. I signal to Bindi, then draw a love heart in the air and point from Bindi to Bhoomi.

"**I love you!**" Bindi blurts out. Bhoomi looks **horrified**.

"**What?** Is this a joke? Look, I don't have time for this, either you have the earring or you don't. I don't think you do, so I'm out of here." I signal wildly to Aunty Bindi. *You've got to stop her from leaving!*

"I…I meant…I love your work," Aunty Bindi finally says. "I think you're very **clever**. I couldn't have come up with a plan like this."

Bhoomi snorts. "Well, most people have very small brains. People **always** underestimate me. That's their **first** mistake."

Bindi looks over at us. I give her an encouraging thumbs up. *Keep going!*

"Well, I think you're **brilliant**. I would have loved to have stolen that diamond – I thought about it plenty, but the museum had one of us security guards sitting there all the time. How did you get past my colleague? He might lose his job, you know."

Bhoomi sneers. "He shouldn't have been so eager to eat a piece of my special mithai, home-made and laced with laxatives. It sent him running to the toilets and nicely out of my way!"

Yes! She's basically just admitted that's how she got rid of the security guard, I think to myself. She's incriminating herself on camera!

"Now, where's my earring?" she demands, stepping forward **threateningly**. "You were not very smart coming here alone."

"Who said I'm here **alone**?" Bindi smiles under the cap.

And that's when we burst out of our hiding place. Milo flicks the light on and we all shout, "**FREEZE!**"

At the same time in bursts a line of **grannies** led by Kangana and Samosa the dog. Bhoomi gets knocked to the floor in the rush of people. They stand shoulder to shoulder, blocking the exit. Behind them I can see a couple of police officers and Parvesh.

"What is this? A grannies' meeting?" Bhoomi scoffs, picking herself up.

Kangana steps forward. "This is the **SHSG**.
And you are in **BIG** trouble!"

Bhoomi glares and for a split second she looks
angry, but she quickly resets her face into a smile.

"Now what is this? You **scared** me!" she says
sweetly.

"You might as well give it up, Bhoomi, we know
everything," I say, folding my arms

"We have you on tape admitting you gave
the guard a laxative to make him leave his post.

It's clear you stole the diamond. Why don't you just tell us where you hid it?"

Bhoomi stares at us and laughs. "I don't have a **clue** what you're talking about. Now look, I've tried to be nice about this, but you really must get out of my way." She tries to push past us.

Suddenly, Aunty Bindi springs to action, taking her hat off and swinging her hair loose dramatically like she's in a shampoo advert. She grabs Bhoomi by the arm and says,

"YOU'RE NOT GOING ANYWHERE!!"

CHAPTER TWENTY

FOUND!

"You **fools** will regret this!" Bhoomi crows trying
to wriggle free as two officers step forward to help
restrain her. "If I stole the jewel, where is it? Without
it, you can't prove anything!"

We all look at each other. She's right – we
STILL don't know where the jewel is.

Just then, Samosa starts barking at Bhoomi.

"What is it, girl?" Milo bends down so he's level
with her. "I think she knows something." He smiles.
"She says she can smell it."

"Dogs do have a **brilliant** sense of smell. Maybe
we need a sniffer dog in here," suggests Kangana.

"No, Samosa can do this," Milo says. He looks

at the dog and tells her, "You've got this, I believe in you." Samosa licks his face and takes a treat from his hand. Then the dog **sniffs** Bhoomi and whines.

Bhoomi screws up her nose in **disgust**. "This is **ridiculous**. How long are we going to stand here and watch this? I have a show to prepare for – the evening acts are waiting to go on!" she says, still trying to shake loose from Aunty Bindi's grip.

Samosa **growls** at Bhoomi and, to our surprise, **jumps** up at her.

Bhoomi **squeals**, horrified. "Get it away from me!"

Samosa continues jumping up at Bhoomi and manages to knock her chunni off.

"Maybe we should **calm** her down, Milo?

She does seem to be getting a **bit** carried away," Parvesh says **nervously**.

Milo steps forward but the dog jumps up one last time and, as Bhoomi tries to bat her away, Samosa **grabs** the headset with her **teeth**, **wrestling** it off Bhoomi.

"It's not a toy, girl!" Milo scolds.

"That's mine! How dare your mangy dog do that! **Give it back**!" Bhoomi tries to fling herself forward to grab the headset, but is restrained by the police officers.

219

Samosa **growls** at her and **nudges** the headset on the floor. And that's when I notice it – a **glint** of something shiny in the earphone of Bhoomi's headset. It couldn't be, **could it**?

We all look at each other.

"So **this** is where you hid it, right in view of everyone!" I say, picking up the headset. I shake it and there's definitely something rattling in the earphone that shouldn't be there.

I peel back the foam padding to reveal...

THE DIAMOND!

We found it!

Bhoomi begins to cry **bitterly**. "I never intended for your granny to be arrested – but it was the perfect cover. How was **I** supposed to know there was an **army of grannies** and a bunch of **nosy kids** on the loose? My plan was **solid**. This would have been my **last hurrah** – one last job and then retirement in Monaco like I always planned. I've had a long **successful** career going from place to place with my event organizer job as a cover. No one ever suspected me till you **kids** came along with your nosy **dog**."

Just then, the detective who arrested Granny Jas comes in with Mum and Dad and Uncle Tony. I'm so glad they got here in time to hear this. I look at the detective hopefully.

She nods at us and then looks at Bhoomi. "No more **jewel-stealing** for you, Bhoomi Biddum! I'd be interested to hear more about all these **other** thefts you've committed too!"

We all **whoop** and jump up and down. Even Samosa runs round in circles, leaping and barking happily. Out of the corner of my eye, I see Bhoomi **glowering** at us.

"You pesky kids and those ghastly grannies! My plan was **perfect!** You all think you're so **clever**. But I will be back! I'll show you! **You'll see!**"

I shudder while she screeches, even as the police officers walk her to the squad car waiting outside.

And then she's **gone**.

We did it! We solved the mystery of the missing diamond. Granny Jas can come home with us!

"Anisha, it's over. We proved Granny's innocence!" Mindy cheers.

"I can't wait to see her!" Milo claps excitedly.

I can't believe it, we really did it. "Let's go," I say. "Let's get Granny out of there!"

CHAPTER TWENTY-ONE
GRANNY'S FREE!

After Officer Winston and the other police officers have taken Bhoomi away, we walk round to the police station, chattering **excitedly**. Aunty Bindi is all emotional and keeps hugging me. Dad says how proud he is of us all, but also tells us off for taking it upon ourselves to conduct an investigation.

"I'm not raising **vigilantes**!" he says.

Mum tells him to stop overreacting. Kangana tells them how **amazing** she thinks we all are. Samosa trots along happily with us, while Milo throws her treats the whole way.

223

When we get to the police station Officer Winston comes to meet us. "I just want to say once again how **sorry** we are about all of this. We're so **pleased** it's been cleared up now. Although I have to tell you, quite a few of our officers have grown rather **attached** to your mum."

We go inside the police station and are led through some double doors. I'm expecting to see poor Granny locked up in a cell, sad and alone. But, oh no, not my granny.

Granny Jas is in a meeting room with glass walls. The door's wide open and with Granny are three young-looking officers. It looks like she's giving them a lecture. She's waggling her finger and now she's demonstrating how to handcuff someone.

"Um, is she allowed to do that?" I ask. "I thought she was under arrest?"

"Ha, well technically she was, but she isn't any more and, I have to say, your granny is **some** lady!" Officer Winston tells me. "We got to talking and it

224

seems she has quite a lot of **experience**. She even offered to help us train some of the new recruits."

"Wow!" Milo and Manny say at the same time.

"I knew Granny was cool, but this is something else." Mindy whistles, impressed.

Meanwhile, I'm thinking, **What kind of experience does my granny have?**

We run into the room and hug Granny as she's mid defence pose. Then we're all jumping up and down, whooping and hugging and high-fiving each other. Granny is **free**! I'm so relieved.

"Granny, you're coming home! I'm so glad.
I knew they'd realize they'd made a mistake," I say,
drinking in the smell of her – spices and olive oil.

"All thanks to you children!" Granny **winks**.
"I heard what you did. With some **special** help,
I believe!" She grins at Kangana, who is standing
by the door. Kangana gives a small nod and a smile.

"Yes, we have lots to catch up on," I say.

"And who is this?" Granny
asks as she bends down to
pat Samosa.

"She's mine," Milo
answers proudly.

"Well, we need to
talk about that,"
interrupts Dad.
"I think we
might have
to find her
a home.

226

I don't think your mum will allow another pet, Milo."

Milo frowns. "Really? But she's so **lovely** and she doesn't smell **that** much any more." He leans down and puts his ear to Samosa. "She says, what will happen to her if I don't look after her?"

Kangana comes forward. "Maybe the **SHSG** could use a detective dog, Milo? She was very **clever** back there and she obviously has a good nose. We'd make sure she has a warm bed and lots of treats," she offers. Samosa licks her hand and wags her tail.

"I think she likes you," Milo says. He leans down to Samosa and whispers in her ear and then listens as she licks his face. "I know, I'd love you to come home with me," he says to her, "but Anisha's dad is right. Mum will never agree to me having another pet and you can do some real good here. We'll keep in touch, **right**?" he asks Samosa hopefully.

Samosa places her paw in his hand as if to say, **friends for ever**.

Milo rubs his eye and looks up at us all. "I've spoken to Samosa, and I guess that would be okay. But you have to promise to FaceTime at least once a week? And email?" Milo asks.

Kangana laughs. "You know I don't like all that **technobobbly** stuff but, for you, Milo, I'll give it a go." Then she turns to Granny Jas and says, "You have a very determined granddaughter there. Keep in touch. Maybe when you get back to Birmingham, we can talk about a Brummie branch of the **SHSG**." And she winks at me.

Granny Jas chuckles. "**Maybe!**"

Then something occurs to me. "Granny, just **one** thing. What **exactly** were you doing at the jewellery exhibition in the first place? You said you were going shopping for spices," I say.

"Well, **beta**, I saw the sign for the museum and Mindy had been saying how **wonderful** this diamond was, so I thought I would check it out. You kids aren't the only ones who like **exploring**, you know!" Granny Jas puts her arm round me. "Now, shall we go? I hear the festival is very good. Maybe we could have a little look for an hour."

Dad frowns, concerned. "Are you sure you wouldn't like a lie-down, Mum? You've had quite an ordeal."

Granny Jas bats him away. "Don't treat me like a **fragile** ornament, **beta**, I'm perfectly fine. I need fresh air. I need to get out and about, not be cooped up at the B & B. We came to Leicester for Anni's Space Centre trip, but that isn't till tomorrow. So in the meantime, I would like to go and see the festival, if that's okay with you!"

Dad backs off. "Alright, alright, you're the **boss**!" he laughs.

As we head out of the police station, a young officer comes up to Granny and says something I can't hear.

"Yes, well just **remember** what I said. Keep your enemy in sight at all times," Granny answers with a wink.

Milo and I look at each other in **surprise**.

Then Granny turns to Officer Winston and says, "Let me write down that paratha recipe for you. It's very easy, **beta**."

I smile then. Even after being arrested and staying the night in a police station, my granny has made all of the officers her **bete** as well.

Once outside, I hug Granny. I'm so glad this is over.

Kangana hugs us both too. "You are one brave

cookie," she tells me. "Consider yourself an honorary member of the **SHSG** – you and all your friends. Right, I'd better get back to the mandir, lots of work to be done," she says. "Come on, Samosa, let's go home. We'll see you all at breakfast before you head off on your trip!" Samosa wags her tail again and off they go.

We all spend the rest of the evening at the side of the festival stage. With Bhoomi gone, Parvesh is in charge and the festival is glorious. There are **fireworks** and food and, best of all, the **BOLLYDREAMERS** perform again! Parvesh gets us passes to go behind the scenes and the band pull Aunty Bindi onstage. Of course, she really gets into it with the backing dancers. She tries to get Uncle Tony to join her, but he hides behind Dad.

Then there's an exciting moment when Parvesh

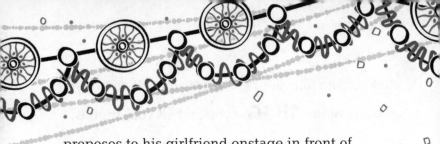

proposes to his girlfriend onstage in front of everyone! A big confetti cannon goes off as she says yes and they hug and kiss. I don't normally like soppy stuff, but it's lovely to see Parvesh so happy. Funny how when we first met him he was so stroppy but I guess working with Bhoomi brought out the worst in him. He's actually a pretty nice person.

Meanwhile Mum makes friends with a few people in the crowd and starts a meditation

circle right there on the ground. Rhadika, the Bollydreamers' manager, comes over to say hello to Granny Jas and they talk for ages, laughing about our big granny mix-up.

"You see, everyone wants to be a granny! But not all grannies are the same, **beta**." Granny Jas chuckles.

"I know," I say, hugging her. "Mine is one of a kind."

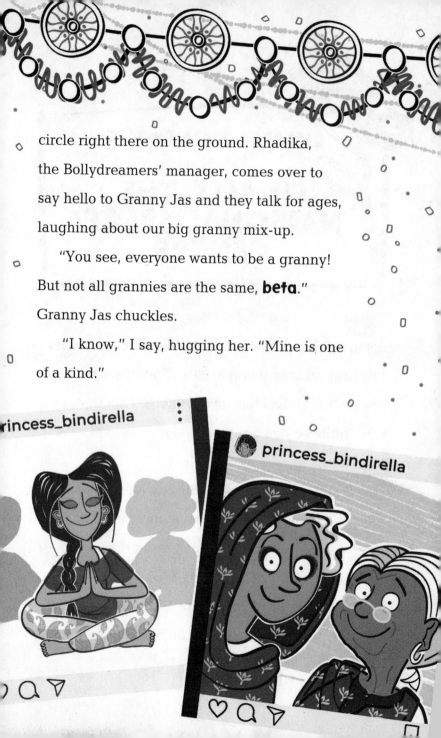

CHAPTER TWENTY-TWO

FINALLY, THE NATIONAL SPACE CENTRE

The next morning it's Monday – the day we finally get to visit the **National Space Centre**. Honestly, I've been so busy trying to clear Granny's name, I haven't even had time to get **excited** about it. I can't **believe** how bonkers the last couple of days have been.

We say an emotional goodbye to Kangana and Samosa. Granny waits till Dad is out of earshot and then promises she'll be in touch about the Birmingham branch of the **SHSG**.

Once we've loaded up all of Aunty Bindi's pink luggage, we get back on the minibus again. Dad switches on the satnav and double-checks the postcode this time. Manny, Milo, Mindy and I all sit together. As we head out on the road, I sit back in my seat with a happy sigh.

"We did it, Neesh. We're **finally** going to see the Space Centre! Are you **excited**?" Milo asks me.

"**I can't wait**!" I grin.

Half an hour later and we are finally there. It's **amazing**, even from the outside. It has a huge spiralling glass dome coming out of the building, and I can see a space rocket pointing towards the sky inside.

"Shall we go in, Anni? Milo? There'll be someone waiting to meet you," Mum says gently.

Suddenly I feel really nervous. "What if I say something **silly**?" I say.

"Never!" says Granny Jas, linking her arm with mine.

"We'll be with you." Mindy smiles, linking Granny's other arm.

And so I take a big, deep **breath** and in we go.

At the reception desk we tell them our names and are given special gold lanyards with badges at the end of them. Mine says **ANISHA MISTRY, PRIZEWINNER!** And Milo's says **MILO MOON, PRIZEWINNER!** too.

We wait for someone to come and collect us. That someone is the Space Centre special visits co-ordinator. She is a small woman with big curly hair that bounces as she walks towards us.

"Hi, I'm Shanice," she says cheerily. "You must be Anisha. And you must be Milo. We've been so excited for your arrival."

I smile, going a little **hot** in the cheeks. I'm not used to being the centre of attention. I usually do everything I can to get out of it! But this is important and special, so I take a deep breath as Milo grabs my hand and, side by side, we follow Shanice, with all my family trailing behind us. We walk up a stairway onto a glass bridge which overlooks some of the exhibits.

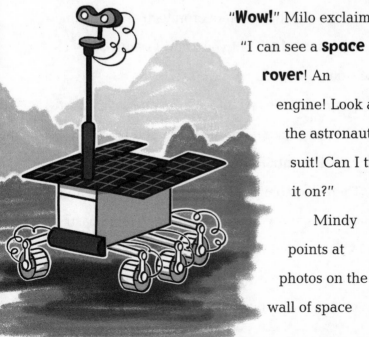

"**Wow!**" Milo exclaims. "I can see a **space rover**! An engine! Look at the astronaut suit! Can I try it on?"

Mindy points at photos on the wall of space

expeditions that happened in the past, while Manny whistles at the model planets hanging from the ceiling. Uncle Tony tries to explain what things are, but I'm not sure he has all his **facts** right. Aunty Bindi corrects him, which makes me smile. I guess she does listen when I tell her stuff about space.

Mum, Dad and Granny Jas wander slowly behind us. Dad keeps asking Granny if she needs to take a break and rest for a minute, but she waves him away. I think he's feeling a bit overprotective of her since she was **arrested**, but you know Granny Jas – she's not having any of it.

Shanice guides us into a room and says, "Just wait here a moment and help yourself to snacks," which is like **music** to Milo's ears.

There's a table filled with crisps and cake and sandwiches and yummy-looking vegetable pastries. Milo, Mindy and Manny all tuck in. Dad hovers by the table and helps himself too. Mum and Granny Jas sit down with their snacks and carry on talking with Uncle Tony and Aunty Bindi. I can't eat anything and I don't really want to talk. I'm too nervous, so I just clutch my autograph book.

"Anni, are you okay? You've gone a little pale, **beta**," Dad comments.

"I'm okay," I **lie**.

Just then the door opens and Shanice comes in, followed by an Indian lady in a salwar kameez. I think to myself, **Is that her?** She looks different from her photo.

239

"Anisha Mistry and Milo Moon, meet Sangeeta Sanśōdhaka!" Shanice announces.

Milo and I step forward and put our hands out to shake hers, but Sangeeta laughs and grabs us in a hug.

"Well done, **bete**! I was so **excited** to hear about your science fair, although I understand you had some mishaps along the way?"

Milo and I blush. "Well…"

She laughs some more. "Do you know how many times we get things wrong in our experiments before we get them right? That's the life of a scientist."

I never thought of it like that before. I make a mental note to write that down later.

"Let's sit. Tell me all about yourselves. Is this your family?" Sangeeta goes over to Mum and Dad and Granny and hugs them. "You must be very proud," she says and they nod, **dumbfounded**.

"And who is this?" She gestures to Mindy and Manny, who are lurking by the food. Manny has half a pastry in his mouth.

"These are my cousins, Mindy and Manny," I say, and Sangeeta hugs them as well.

We all sit down and she spends time talking to everyone. It feels like we've known her for ever. Granny Jas chats away to her as if she's another one of her bete.

"You're thinking I seem **normal**, right?" Sangeeta chuckles, catching me staring at her. She nudges me and whispers, "I'll let you into a secret. I **am** normal. Well, as normal as anyone else. I'm a mum and a wife, but I also happen to have helped launch a rover into space that went to Mars. That could be you one day. There's no special ingredient for success, beta. You can be **anything**. Actually, scrap that, you can be more than one thing, you could be **all** the things!" She chuckles.

"I love science," I admit. "But I don't know if I have what it takes to be a proper scientist."

"Well, I hear you are a **very** determined person," Sangeeta replies, winking at Granny Jas, who has obviously been filling her in on my mystery-solving escapades. "And there is more than one job in the field of science. I'm sure we could use your very special skill set in the industry. You know, there is a **space camp** we run in America for **gifted** children," she says. "Would you be up for that?"

Dad overhears (because he's **eavesdropping**!) and comes to sit with us.

"I've always fancied a family trip to America. They have those great big Winnebagos. Like our minibus but even **BIGGER**! I think I'd be good at driving one of those. We could take the whole family."

"Well, before you start booking flights, Mr Mistry, I was **actually** thinking of running one over here in the UK. If we can find more talent like Anisha's, then it would definitely be worth it. I'll take your details and we'll keep in touch."

Inside, I'm doing **somersaults**, because Sangeeta Sanśōdhaka wants to keep in touch with me! Outwardly, I just nod and smile, like it's the most **chill** thing in the world.

We get a chance to ask more questions about her work and I have a whole list.

"If you weren't a space engineer, what would you be?" I ask. "Was there **another** job you thought you'd be good at?"

Sangeeta smiles. "Actually, yes, I really wanted to be a **librarian** when I was growing up. I love books so much. But I also love animals, so at one point I thought I would quite like to be a **vet**. I guess I found my way to my true calling in the end but, who knows? I could have been something else entirely."

Granny leans in. "Did you know, when I was a girl, I really wanted to be a **pilot** or a **spy**?"

I laugh. "I can believe that Granny."

Mum joins in. "I wanted to be a **dancer**. I used to learn traditional Indian dance, you know." She dips with her knees bent and hands in a prayer position.

Dad adds, "I told you I wanted to be a **gymnast**, didn't I? I also had dreams of being a champion **tennis player**. I was quite good in my day." He swings an imaginary racket. "But then I found the law and I knew I wanted to spend my days helping people. It's the best feeling."

Uncle Tony joins in. "I was going to be a **cricketer**, except I wasn't very good at it." He laughs. "But then I started my own little business selling old phones and I really enjoyed being my own **boss**."

"I wanted to be a **beautician** for a while," says Aunty Bindi, "but my big dream was to be on the telly. I always thought I'd make a great **TV host**. I do like helping Tony run the business now, but I'd quite like my own party-planning company. I think I'd be good at that."

Uncle Tony holds her hand. "You'll be better than good. I think you should do it."

"I want to be a **vet**," says Milo very certainly.

"I don't know what I want to be," Mindy puts in quietly.

"That's okay, **beta**. You have lots of time to figure that out and have fun trying different things in the meantime." Sangeeta smiles.

"I know what I want to be," Manny says. "An entrepreneur, like my dad. Or I'm going to **invent** something really cool. I don't know **what** yet, but's going to be **awesome**!"

Everyone laughs and agrees that whatever it, it will surely be brilliant.

We get a special tour of the Space Centre n Sangeeta then. We get to do loads of fun stuke

sitting in a real-life rocket that has actually been to space. We look at a proper space computer and try to stop Milo from pressing every button. We sit in the planetarium, which is basically a big theatre with a huge screen that goes right over your head. It's really beautiful when the show starts,

because it feels just like we're in space, whizzing past earth, the moon and beyond. It's the most amazing thing I've ever seen. I lean back and lose myself in the stars. It's the first time everyone in my family has ever been this quiet.

A little while later we have a break. Sangeeta goes off to have some photographs taken, while we make the most of the opportunity to have a snack. Granny hands me a Tupperware box filled with treats by Kangana before we left. The smell of pakora and tandoori chicken pieces is delicious. Granny smiles as I tuck in.

"I know you love science and space, **beta**, but you know, you really saved me this weekend. Have you ever considered a career as a detective?" Granny asks. "Like Sangeeta says, you can be more than one thing. You can achieve *so* many things!"

"No," I laugh. "I'm not a detective. I just have a way of looking at things logically, that's all."

"You could do both – be a science detective!" Milo grins as he plonks himself next to me.

I think about it...

Science detective...

Yeah, that could be **COOL**!

Just then, a man in a National Space Centre T-shirt runs over.

"Are you that girl who found the stolen diamond over at the museum?" he asks.

"Um…yes," I reply hesitantly.

"I hope you don't mind me interrupting, but we have an **emergency**. It's a real scientific mystery and no one can figure out what's happened," he explains.

Granny and Milo look at me expectantly as I think for a second.

You know, maybe I **can** help, like I helped Granny Jas.

I look at the man and reply, "Tell me everything."

ANISHA

+

A LITTLE HELP FROM
MY FRIENDS

=

CASE SOLVED

MEET RITU KARIDHAL,

Rocket Woman
of India, and the
real-life inspiration for
the fictional character of
Sangeeta Sanśōdhaka.

In *Granny Trouble*, Anisha cannot wait to meet
famous Indian space engineer, Sangeeta
Sanśōdhaka, at the National Space Centre. After all,
Sangeeta has Anisha's dream job! Sangeeta
Sanśōdhaka is not a real person, but her character
was inspired by a real-life Indian aerospace
engineer, Ritu Karidhal.

As a little girl growing up in the Indian city of
Lucknow, Ritu loved to stargaze, marvelling at the
night sky above. As she grew older, she regularly
checked the newspapers for any information related

to space science, and made sure she stayed up-to-date on the work of NASA (National Aeronautics and Space Administration) and ISRO (Indian Space Research Organisation).

Ritu worked hard and followed her dreams with determination. After studying physics at university, she applied for a job at ISRO, and was accepted. In 2007, Ritu received the ISRO Young Scientist Award from the president of India.

Ritu went on to play a very important part in India's mission to Mars, which launched in November 2013. India became the fourth country in the world to reach Mars, and the first country to reach the Red Planet on its initial attempt. The mission was one of the ISRO's most significant achievements.

Ritu is known as one of the celebrated Rocket Women of India who worked on the Mars Orbiter Mission (aka MOM). She has inspired a whole generation of young girls to follow their dreams.

MEET THE AUTHOR

Name: Serena Kumari Patel

Lives with: My brilliant family, Deepak, Alyssa and Reiss

Favourite Subjects: Science and History

Ambitions: To learn to ride a bike (I never learned as a kid).

To keep trying things I'm scared of.

To write lots more books.

Most embarrassing moment:

Singing in Hindi at a talent show and getting most of the words wrong. I hid in the loo after!

MEET THE ILLUSTRATOR

Name: Emma Jane McCann

Lives with: A mysterious Tea Wizard called Granny Goddy, a family of bats in the attic, and far too many spiders. (I promise I'm not a witch.)

Favourite thing to draw: Spooky stuff like Dracula's Den in Anisha's first adventure. (Still not a witch, honest.)

Ambitions: To master a convincing slow foxtrot.

Most embarrassing moment:

I used to collect old teacups and china. One day, I was in a teashop with a friend and the cup she was using was really pretty. I picked it up to check the maker's mark on the base, forgot it already had tea in it, and spilled the lot all over the both of us. (Witches are too cool to ever do anything like that.)

ACKNOWLEDGEMENTS

It seems strange to be writing my third set of acknowledgements in two years. I can't believe the journey my books and I have been on and there is so much more yet to come. I am supported by the most incredibly generous and talented team and I feel very lucky to have so many strong and brilliant women involved with my writing career. To them I say thank you a million times. To Kate Shaw for all her agenting expertise and for just being generally wonderful. To Stephanie King, the best editor I could have hoped for. Alice Moloney for jumping into Anisha's world and making it all the better. Huge thanks to Emma McCann for bringing so much warmth and fun to the books with your amazing illustrations. Special thanks to Kat, Fritha, Stevie, Will and everyone at Usborne who helps to make the Anisha series, I am so grateful for you all.

I want to thank a few special people who I only know through Twitter, which might seem like a strange thing to do. But their support of this series has meant a lot and I really believe it has made such a difference. Robin Stevens, Dionne Lakey, Scott Evans, Ashley Booth, Rumena Akhtar, Mita Mistry, Emily Drabble and everyone at BookTrust. Every teacher, librarian, blogger and bookseller who has read, reviewed or recommended the books, you have my heartfelt gratitude. To the USBAH teams thank you for welcoming me so warmly and for everything you do to put these books into the hands of readers. I really never knew or believed how far Anisha's stories could go and it's your warmth and enthusiasm that has carried me through this past year.

To the swaggers, you know who you are, thank you for lifting me up when I'm down, for making me belly laugh and for always giving me much needed perspective!

To every fellow author who has offered support or a kind word, I appreciate it so much, thank you for making me feel part of a community. Special thanks to Rikin Parekh for a very random twitter conversation which sparked the idea for the SHSG.

And so, to my family and friends who continue to cheer me on, celebrate every small win with me, tell everyone they know about the books and either make them buy it or inflict it upon their children as a gift. Your excitement and pride in what we're achieving is one of the best things about all this.

Lastly my precious ones, like many families we four amigos have had a huge amount of enforced quality time together recently and (aside from the odd Monopoly related squabble) we still find things to smile about. You are my joy, my loves, my everything.

Look out for the fourth
fabulously funny adventure from

ANISHA
ACCIDENTAL DETECTIVE

SHOW STOPPERS!

"I'm SO stressed!!
Our class is putting on a
musical, and we only have ONE WEEK to
organize everything! I'm leaving the theatrics
to Milo, but as the director's assistant I have
LOADS to do…especially as everything is going
wrong! The costumes, the sets…even Molly the
cat is forgetting her cues. Miss Jive thinks the
show is CURSED, but I smell sabotage.
It's time for me, Anisha, Accidental Detective,
to step into the spotlight and save the show!"